I0618382

First Edition
ISBN 978-0-9912283-6-2
Tiny Mind Creative
1270 Caroline Street
Suite D120-331
Atlanta GA 30307
www.tinymind.com

Part I
The Making of a god

The birth was extraordinarily traumatic, lasting until his mother was gasping towards her last breaths in wracked pain. He would leave her crippled for the remainder of her life, but he burst from her strong on that sweltering summer night, screeching to the world that he had arrived.

Aquilla was born on the plantation of Obediah Stafford in Milledgeville Georgia May 1, 1848. His father spared little love for his son, who nearly split his mother in two during birth. Obediah had courted Francine for years before they were married. She held her back in perfect posture and knew the eyes of all followed her as she walked the streets. Her long red-brown her was always pinned up beneath a fashionable hat that suited her better than it could any other women. In a dress, she was a vision, tight at her waist showcasing a slim yet shapely figure. She was the only light of his life, all the work he had done to build up his fortune was solely to impress her father and allow him to ask for her hand. The day they wed was pinnacle of his life. He'd praised God in all his bountiful compassion for blessing him with everything any man could want for. The marriage was joyous and they delighted in each other's company. They held and attended endless social parties and could never bear to stray out of sight of one another in mixed company. The hand of one would search for the hand of the other, caressing the palm of their beloved gently, devotedly. They would sink deep into each other's eyes and feel the need to bid their goodbye from their friends. In the carriage ride home Obediah couldn't keep his hands off of her until she would beg him to stop for the gossip of the driver.

For all this passion and yearning they were at a loss to bear a child. As time slipped by, the stress of this weighed heavily on Obediah for, though he himself wanted for an heir, he saw the ache for a baby oppress her mood more and more. She would visit the slave women who had given birth to hold their infants and return to the mansion collapsing in her couch drenched in tears. Obediah prayed to the same God that had blessed him so through his life, "Why abandon me now? What have I done to betray or anger you that you cannot give your holy gift of an infant for my trembling wife?"

As time went on, Obediah grew dark and short tempered. He would take long strolls alone through his fields and lands, not responding to any hails from his slaves and workmen. On one of these walks, Obediah sat above the stream on a fallen tree that crossed it, staring down in the sparkling stars within the bubbling waters reflecting the setting sun. Souza, one of the house slaves, approached him gently to sooth him mind. She always knew how to calm him when agitation struck his spirit. Souza was in her early 20s and displayed an elegance and grace that demanded respect even from her position. He listen quietly to her now as she worked her serene magic. She spoke of an elixir that was used in her homeland to increase fertility in couples that found difficulty having children. She promised him a strong male heir would come from their union that night if they both but drank of it. He looked at her, spouting madness, wanting to call her on her dementia that a potion would solve his plight. But her eyes calmed him with their kindness and her gentle hand caressing his back won him over. She held his arm as they walked back in the darkening onset of evening. The fireflies began to shine out and he felt a bit of peace that has escaped him for some time. They entered the house and she went to prepare the tonics. He sought out Francine, brooded in dim candlelight upon her couch. Her eyes looked miles away, softly sullen, as if all effort was spent on getting her disposition to this elevation; it was all she could do to maintain such composure. He sat down beside her and cupped her hands between both of his. "Francine darling." She didn't respond, she was far off lost in thought, not even aware of his presence or touch. Gently he caressed her hand, patient for her to return to him. At time, she did, looking first at her hand amidst his, and then at his eyes flowing care and devotion towards her. She smiled and leaned herself against him to be held.

"I know we should try again tonight my pet. I just can't find the strength within me to even make it up the stairs."

"Then I shall carry you my dove. For tonight I foresee a miracle. A miracle of miracles heavenly sent just for you and I. I can hear the stork on wing now, searching the night sky for the Stafford home."

She laughed and brightened with his jokes and good spirit. He helped return her color. Souza entered with the drinks, placing them on the coffee table before them. "What is this Souza?" Francine asked picking up the glass and smelling it. The odor was sharp and unfamiliar.

"This is a gift from me to the two of you on your journey to bear a child. This drink never fails in all the years it has been used."

Francine trusted Souza, but was concerned about taking such a strong smelling drink in her weakened state. "I appreciate your kindness, but I fear my temperament is unprepared for the hardiness of your brew."

"Do not be concerned so, it will give you both energy and tranquility. You will be open to the journey of bringing your child into the world. That is the purpose of the drink, to free the pathways that have been blocked."

Obediah downed his drink soundly and tapped the glass on the table to show his firm support to Souza's offer. Francine looked at him in wonder, curious at the remarkable mood everyone was exhibiting tonight. She laughed half-heartedly and lifted the glass to her lips. The taste seemed sour, but was masked by heavy licorice and alcohol. She stopped after the first sip and nearly gagged.

"You must drink it all, I made just enough for both of you."

Francine looked at Souza and then Obediah and lifted the glass once again, this time trying not to breath, drinking it as quickly as she was able, a sour unhappy look across her face as she did so. Once finished, she felt a need to retch and bring it back up, but she fought this and wiped her mouth with her handkerchief.

It took very little time to hit them. They hadn't noticed when Souza had left the room. She had lit additional candles before doing so, and their fragrance was desirous. They both breathed the sensual aroma in and felt warmth all over their bodies, especially in their hands, their chests and their loins. Obediah lifted Francine in his arms and carried her from the day room and up the staircase to their bedroom. There were more candles around the bed as well. By this time, Francine was tugging at the ties and buttons of her dress, desperately needing to be free of it. The slightest glimpse of her pink chest bred a fire within Obediah that could not be quenched. He threw her upon the bed and tore the dress in shreds from her. Francine's eyed him widely and with exhilaration, he felt a level of bursting manhood that he never before experienced. He stripped himself as well, standing before the bed breathing heavily and fully erect. Her body drew him with a lust that overpowered and consumed his previous affections. He pulled her up by her arm and slapped her full on with the back of his hand, her nose and lip flowing in reaction. She swooned from it and he struck her again and again. She moaned and her body arched achingly. He placed his hand between her legs and felt her engorged and flowing like fresh sap. He entered her with a thrust and she screamed scratching her nails deep into his ass and drawing blood, pushing him ever deeper within her. They fought and struggled to fulfill their endless appetites throughout the night, finally collapsing in sheer exhaustion once the last of the candles had gone out.

The child had been conceived.

Aquilla loved his mother, but felt no affection for his father, who blamed him for taking all the vitality from Francine when they pulled him from her body. The scowl Obediah bore across the dinner table, while his mother had to be specially fed at her bed by Souza. He rarely addressed the boy other than the send him to his room when Aquilla lingered too close while Obediah was smoking and reading in his study. At times, Obediah would drown his frustration in bourbon and Aquilla learned to keep clear during these nights or chance a confrontation with the full wrath of his father. "Boy! Come here!" He'd grab his son by the ear and stare at him with eyes filled with drunken rage. "Why could you not have been born peacefully? Why did you have to lame her, you worthless scourge!?" Aquilla would free himself and run crying to his mother, begging her forgiveness which she assured him there was no need of. Her beautiful son was all she could ask for.

The slave Dapney raised him and he had great love for her kindness and affection. It was Dapney and the slaves that taught him the skills that fascinated him most. Hunting, fighting, chasing, climbing. He was a natural at anything he found an eye for and was drawn to playmates that were able to keep up with him. But he was most drawn the Clarissa. She was a year older than him, born a slave to Dapney's daughter. She was lithe, elegant and breathtaking to behold. He had first been taken by her smile when he was chasing some of the boys around the barn and nearly ran into her as she carried a pail of water. He dislodged the pail from her and slipped into the muck at her feet face-first. She laughed in a comely way that made him forget about his game. She fetched more water and cleaned the mud from his face with her hand. The touch of her hand across his face brought warm strong sensations he was not familiar with at that age. He began to adore her. The brightness of her eyes. The gorgeous flow of her long dark hair. They spent much time together after this encounter talking and smiling to one another. As the years passed and he reached 15 years, many girls in town showed interest in him, but none of them could capture his attention like Clarissa. He had grown in those few years from a fast strong child full of energy to a buck of a young man with striking features and a fire that drew the attention of everyone he passed. His father could not help but be proud of him. There were times when he wished to run out and grab the boy up and tell him how he felt, but these moments didn't last. His wife's beauty, the only thing to have survived the violence of Aquilla's exit from her, had slowly faded and he now could not even remember what he first saw in her. He only recalled that she had been his world, his entire reason for being, the purpose for which he poured his soul out in his ingenuity and passions each day. And it was his no longer. He saw his son with Clarissa from the second floor window of the manor near the bedroom where his sickly wife lay. He recognized the adoration in both their eyes. It gnawed at him – a jealousy bred of complex emotions. An unfair rage that the son who had taken his love away from him should have his own. An outrage that the boy's affections should turn to a slave of all things! But most of all, the unfairness and pain of seeing the two of them sharing the same tranquility and exhilaration that he had worked his entire life to earn for himself, only to lose so very quickly. These two, they want for nothing. The boy pours no labor into earning her affection or the respect of her father. It all comes naturally as a gift from God. He struck out with his hand in frustration and shattered a lamp on the table beside him. It cut deep into his hand and he called out for Souza to help him.

"This cut is deep sir, we must dress it." Souza cared for the wound and

Obediah flinched from the ache of it. She soothed him and gave him another of her special elixirs to ease the pain.

Aquilla sat near the stream with Clarissa as the sun made its way down, casting warm glows across her beautiful skin and hair. He pulled off his shirt and bade her to swim with him. She laughed as he dropped his pants and she saw his manhood. They had swam many times before, but as children. She could not keep her eyes off of how he now looked to her. He lifted her by her hands and kissed her generously. They had kissed both in play and true affection, but this kiss she could feel was just a prelude of where they were going tonight. She would not separate from him tonight to dreaming of what it would feel like to have his hands run across her body. He undid her dress and she was naked before him. He lifted her in his strong arms and waded into the water, gently holding her as the waters caressed her. He kissed her again upon the lips and across her cheek and to her neck. She ran her fingers through his hair and let out a small sigh as she reached her mouth hungrily for his and they kissed as they'd never kissed before. They returned to the shore and he laid out their clothes for comfort in the grass, placing her down upon them and easing his way across her figure. Exploring intimately every curve, every muscle, tasting the richness of her skin, memorizing the flavor and feel of her body with his lips and hands. They unified their bond of affection that evening, each giving freely and fully to the other – worshiping, craving, delighting in the physicality of their lover and the passions they yielded one another.

As the half moon crept up the night sky they held each other contently in the breezeless air.

"Are you cold?" He asked her as she snuggled against him.

"Not where I'm touching you."

"Are you thirsty."

"Yes, but I can wait. I'm not ready to let go of you yet my love."

He kissed her deeply not once but three time, caressing her face in his hands. "I won't be long. I'll bring us drinks and blankets. We'll spend the night camped by the water. I want to awake with you in my arms, the bubbling of the stream in my ears and the morning sun in my eyes." She smiled at him warmly as he pulled on his pants and kissed her once more before he raced back down the path towards the house.

Obediah sat in the shadows as his son passed him heading back to the manor. He had taken a walk down the stream to relax his frantic mind, ease the pain in his hand. When he came upon the two, he felt the fire of anger and animal lust. She was as perfect as Francine had been before his son had butchered her. She gave forth the same euphoric moans as they lay together in amorous embrace. He detested it. He deplored it. He wanted to destroy it. He watched as the boy left down the path and crept up to where she lay peacefully listening to the waters. She was singing a song quietly to herself as he made his silent approach upon her. Grabbing her fiercely by the arm he punched her face three times until she went limp. He collected her clothes and threw her over his shoulder taking her further into the forest back to where there was only a small woodshed. Inside the shed he laid her across the dusty table covered in shavings and lowered his pants to force himself within her. He used her unconscious form to expel all the anger and frustration that had built up since his son had mutilated his love. He wish to do the same with Aquilla's love, pounding her face against the table as he rent her vagina with rough brutal slaps and scratches. Taking a rope from the wall he beat her across the back, ass and legs and then tied it around her neck to choke her as he once again mounted her from behind. She fought for consciousness and clawed at the rope but he pulled her arm roughly behind her and punished her harder until he climaxed in a wave of anger, exhilaration, self alienation, panic, and fulfillment. He collapsed on top of her, heaving for breath, blood coursing fresh from his reopened hand across her back mixing with the blood he'd drawn from his lashes upon her.

Uncertain of what to do now, he sat down heavily upon the floor. Clarissa moaned and wept feebly on the table, unable to move. He could not look upon her. He was not sure what he had become. He was not sure if he felt wrong about this or absolutely right. He dusted the shavings from his ass, pulled his trousers back up and headed towards the house, making sure to avoid Aquilla who was out calling her name and searching for her in vain.

He got back to the mansion and Souza was waiting for him. She saw the blood running down his wounded hands, she saw the fire and dementia in his eyes. She brought him back in and re-cleaned his wounds, as well as cleaning the fresh ones on the other hand he had used to beat Clarissa with. He shared with her what he had done. Not caring what judgement she might pass, but having to speak it out to know that it was truth. She listened patiently and told him everything would be fine. She promised she would take care of it immediately. She finished setting his cuts again and ushered him to a couch. She gave him a drink to make him relax and he soon felt drowsy and sank back into the couch asleep.

Souza went out of the mansion and gathered Abraham, Socrates and Lilian. They discussed the best course of action and began implementation immediately. They retrieved Clarissa from the woodshed and wrapped her in a blanket. They carried her off the property into the rocky woods beyond and into a cave. Here they went about nurturing her back to health over several weeks. Feeding her, cleaning and tending her wounds but not allowing her to leave. They gave her medicines meant to aid the healing that made her despondent and uncaring.

Aquilla pleaded with everyone on the plantation for information on Clarissa. No one knew anything or at least were willing to say. He was distraught with anxiety and panic. He was gone such a short time how could she just completely disappear without any evidence of what had befallen her? He went to all the neighboring plantations, he spoke with everyone he could in town if they had seen any sign at all of her.

Obediah had decided to sell her once she had fully recovered, somewhere far away where they would not meet again. After four weeks in the cave, they decided she was ready for travel and prepared her for sale in Atlanta. Souza escorted her into town to board a wagon headed for Atlanta with other slaves meant for sale. She was by far the youngest most beautiful of the group and there was much discussion as to whom she belonged and why she was being sold. Before long she was recognized for who she was and the questioning turned to why Obediah might be so in need of cash he would part with this treasure. Word travelled fast and soon after the wagon headed out towards Atlanta, Aquilla was aware of it. He raced back to the plantation and into the stables for his horse, storming madly down the road as Obediah and the rest of the plantation eyed his fiery receding form.

He chased down the wagon, his horse weary and gasping from the pressured run. He commanded them to stop and fought with the men to have access to their cargo.

"Clarissa! Clarissa!" He cried looking in the bars for her to answer. She did not turn to him, but he finally saw her.

"Clarissa! What is this? Where have you been? I've been searching for you endlessly." She didn't answer, simply staring at her feet.

"Clarissa my love! Speak to me. Have you been okay? Has anything happened to you? Has anyone hurt you? I've been desperate to find you and learn who could have taken you from me."

"I wasn't taken Aquilla. I asked to leave."

Her voice was an instant joy to him, but the words were so harsh, almost seething in a quiet controlled tone. He felt only a flowing wave of disdain for him coming off of her as she continued to stare solidly at the floor below.

"But why? What have I done? How can you abandon what we have —"

"We don't have anything Aquilla!" With this she did look him in the eyes and she burned with prepared venom. "You have what you have and I have nothing. We shared nothing. We are nothing."

"Clarissa that is so untrue! All these years you've never shown me any such face as you are wearing now. Someone has turned you from me and I will make them pay for what they've done to you."

"No one turned me Aquilla. You turned me. You took what you can take because I have no say in it. What you think was kindness from me has always been to protect myself. But I can't protect myself here any more. Not from you or anyone. Goodbye Aquilla, find someone who can truly love you not someone you must force yourself upon."

Devastated by these words, Aquilla fell from the side of the wagon. Unable to maintain his footing he collapsed over on his side, not even catching himself with his arms. His head struck the pebbled road and bled slightly, building a large lump. His world was spinning. His mind screaming in a madness of confusion. How could any of this be true? How could something so perfect be so completely false? How much of his life was set to be beautiful seductive lies that snap and poison his soul with their fangs.

Aquilla spent most of the night at the roadside, contemplating how life had dislodged him fully from childhood, from comfort, from love into a dark friendless wasteland. He knew where his father kept some petty cash, he listed small items he could trade and sell, including his horse. He made plans to leave for good, never look back. There was nothing but pain to surround him in this place. He wanted a different kind of pain. The pain that comes from hard work and exhilarating experiences. He blamed his father for losing Clarissa. He did not know how or why he was involved, but the endless oppressive loathing that Obediah had inundated him with all his life stank in this dark affair.

He crept back to the plantation deep in the night, walking his horse quietly and tying him far from where ears might hear. He crept his way into the manor and collected the goods he felt most applicable for his journey, including anything small that could turn into substantial funds as his mother's jewelry surely would. He dressed and collected the most useful clothes and tools, including his father's pistol, and left the house of his childhood without looking once back at it. He wished it would burn behind him now. Even then he would not turn, but simply enjoy the heat, the wails of despair and the howl of pain as his father burned alive.

In the morning he sold his horse to a gentleman willing to do this without proper paperwork. He bought his way onto a wagon heading towards Savannah. In Savannah he worked various jobs as could be found, mainly unloading ships from distant ports. He tried to befriend as many of the seamen as he could and expressed interest in going off on a voyage of his own. This led to a chance to deck a ship heading for the Gold Coast, an opportunity he jumped at immediately. He watched as the land slowly receded behind him. He had escaped his father. He had escaped the misery of the accursed life that wretched man had preyed upon him. He was his own man now, for once fully in control of his own destiny.

The ship voyage taught him as much about drinking as the sea. He drowned his frustrations and stamped out the buds of his tender childhood dreams in a constant flow of binge alcohol. He learned to fight with his hands in multiple styles of combat. He grew to enjoy the sweat and stench of sea life. The hard work and even harder play suited his disposition well. The ache receded within him and he rebuilt himself anew. He kept the name Aquilla, but refused to give anyone his surname. He told everyone he was a bastard, self-made, angry as hell at the world and not taking shit from anyone. This of course garnered him much respect in the crew. He worked hard, but some doubted his lack of pedigree. His teeth were too good and his hands too soft. A crewman named Everhardt especially seemed suspicious. Aquilla took this attention seriously and requested the captain if he could pay him to stow his goods in his quarters. This was agreed upon and it was shortly later that Aquilla caught Everhardt rifling through what remained of his belongings.

"Find what you were looking for?"

Everhardt startled and turned to him, obviously searching his mind for an excuse. "Someone stole my pipe, I thought it might be you."

"I've never seen your pipe."

"That's because someone stole it!"

"Why would I steal your pipe Everhardt?"

Everhardt smiled at this with a rank scraggly grin. "Because of what I put in it. Would you like to know what it is I put in it?"

Curious where he was going with this Aquilla humored the goat. "Why don't you show me what you put in your pipe Everhardt? Perhaps I will help you find a proper pipe if it interests me."

Everhardt laughed raspily at this wagging his finger at Aquilla. "Oh, you – you will definitely be interested. Meet in the hold an hour after dark and you'll be interested." He continued to laugh and headed out of the cabin.

Aquilla entered the hold at the time set and saw Everhardt on the floor working on his pipe. "I thought you'd lost your pipe. Wasn't that what all the ruckus was about earlier?"

Everhardt just laughed at him from where he sat, a cloud of smoke swirling about him. "I found it." He continued his laughter and issued for Aquilla to join him patting the floor beside him. Aquilla sat and smelled the pungent smoke. It was not tobacco and he was unfamiliar with what it could be. Everhardt passed him the pipe and he inhaled deeply on it and released it. "More slowly this time, don't exhale so quickly mate." Aquilla took another drag from the pipe holding it for a moment before sending out a cloud, this time he coughed uncontrollably. He was used to tobacco, but this felt much different. As the ship sailed on, time wound down, sound itself went slowly. The roll of the ocean waves had a new rhythm to them that seemed to match his mood. He felt peaceful and connected to everything around him. The movement of his breath, the sensitive feeling as he moved his eyes to look around him, all these took a new luscious dimension. Everhardt handed the pipe to him again and he continued this journey. Soon time began to wrap around on itself. He could not be certain when something was happening. Had Everhardt passed him the pipe or was he about to. Did he answer the last question or had the question yet to be asked? These problems of succession became more and more complex and required expanding efforts of his thought to organize. He was aware Everhardt was droning on about something, but he was no longer certain Everhardt was in the same room at the same time as he was. Soon even contemplating sequence was too difficult as the world split from distinct objects into swirling colors and shapes, thoughts and images, glimpses of Clarissa as the Egyptian goddess Isis and his father as a naked burning devil. He grew quieter and drew inward until sleep took him away.

Aquilla spent the next few years in Cape Coast. He started with Everhardt as his companion and they traded the hasheesh to the sailors and city folk able to pay for the rarity. Over time, he grew beyond Everhardt and became known as the prime drug merchant in the coast. The sailors with goods found their way to him. He hired men to protect him and women and children to keep their eyes and ears on the street. He lavished himself with exotic ladies and explored every aspect of pleasure he could attain. By the age of 19 he found himself rich, powerful and insufferably bored. Nothing was ever enough. No matter the drugs, no matter the number of women, it left him cold late at night wanting more from life. Something richer, darker, fiercer.

It was towards this end that fate brought him Olmstead. Elias Olmstead from Connecticut. He'd entered Aquilla's bar and sat down at the poker table. Dressed as a gentleman's gentleman, as many pretenders Aquilla had become familiar with. After several rounds of whiskey and a string of lost games he was about to be tossed out when he begged Aquilla to provide him just a moment of his consideration.

"I understand you are a man of taste and conviction. A man who appreciates the finer things in life as well as the exotic."

"These facts have no bearing on your tab unless you are alluding to something of specific value that can clear your debt to me."

"I believe I do have such an item for a man of your remarkable tastes and keen judgement. To an untrained eye it is just a bauble, but to the eye that can see there is something more. Much more." With this flourish, Olmstead took out a pouch from which he drew a scarab beetle. It wasn't jewelry, it was an actual beetle. It was beautiful in its iridescence and its seamless perfection, but simply a bug.

Aquilla stared at Olmstead awaiting a reason not to have the man's hand chopped off for wasting his time. "Sir, I know what you are thinking. It's simply a beetle, what is my point? The point you see is it is neither alive or not alive." He rolled the scarab over and showed its legs and all its body fully intact clenched tightly together. "Now I acquired this creature some years ago from a moslem trader who insisted it was a magical insect and was all that remained of a devil cult that hailed from deep within Cameroon. For years they were feared and avoided by all their neighbors for their fiendish practices. They would steal livestock as well children and women, and not for slaving, but for their own blood ceremonies. Stories of sex with the dying, mass murders and undead monsters became more and more prevalent about this clan. Eventually, the sacrifices were too much and the surrounding villagers banded together and attacked. They slaughtered everyone, burned everything they could find. They practically torched the area for miles around. The ground was still hot days later when this moslem came across the corpses charred and twisted in agony. Dogs, birds, children, women everything was slain and torched. But he also found an old man sitting alone amidst the smoking wreckage. The man held this scarab and he handed it to the moslem who carried it with him for another six years before he offered it to me. In all this time the beetle has neither moved or decomposed. It exists in a state of waiting."

Aquilla continued to view the man with distain. This story was surely one of great imagination, but all this to sell him a dead bug?

"Look if you will, into its eyes. They have a darkness that defies death. There is a depth in those eyes that at times I have felt looked through me, as if it knew me for what I was. As if it were awaiting something from me."

Aquilla lifted the beetle into his hand and stared into its eyes, taking another draw from his pipe and holding it before blowing across the beetle's face. The eyes. They did seem to have a presence behind them. Either that or this madman was infecting him. He placed the scarab on the table and drew out his knife to stab it. As he swung the blade down, it lifted itself quickly on its legs and stepped away, the knife spearing into the table. It had happened so quickly the bug already was back to its normal position with its legs withdrawn and no sign of life.

"Dearest Mary Mother of God!" Screamed Olmstead leaping from the table both in fear and delight. "Now sir, surely this magnificent insect is meant for your attention! I have never once seen it react to anything, even when I have dropped it on occasion. The scarab was meant to come to your hands sir. I only hope that you will offer me the service of clearing my debt to you this night in return for bringing destiny to your table."

"Get out." Aquilla answered still staring at the scarab.

"Of course sir, of course. I bid you farewell."

Aquilla took another breath from his pipe and again picked up the scarab. He felt an energy from it. He felt a calling. There was an attachment deep inside him to this insect that had been there all along, waiting for today.

11

The quest to find the dead lands the moslem spoke to Olmstead of was a simple one. Aquilla's wealth bought answers and action. He travelled into Cameroon deep into the northern region to a land of permanently scorched earth. It was said that nothing lived in that region ever since the sect of mad sorcerers had been slaughter and their demonic beasts burned. Everyone trekked widely around it and the smell of death still wafted into the nearby forests and valleys. Streams that flowed through that region were considered unsafe for any use. Any livestock that wandered off in that direction was not pursued, but considered permanently lost. It was a hole down to hell in the middle of the jungle. Warnings painted on the trunks of trees approaching the site describe such and reproached to turn back for the sake of your soul and your family's souls. Aquilla went forward into the province of the demised.

Dead birds, insects, lizards, snakes and small mammals were rotting all about him as he entered the circle of devastation. The ground was dry and supported no plants, only dead dried trees stood about him. It smelled of death, a mixture of recent and aged corpses that permeated the area as an abundance of perfume. He took a handkerchief from his pocket and wrapped it about his mouth. He noticed something in his jacket pocket and withdrew the pouch with the scarab. It was moving. He opened the pouch and dropped it upright onto his palm. The creature lifted its ornate shell and took to flight off slightly to the left of his current path. He raced after it to keep up, though it appears to taper its pace to his limitations. He had to weave his way around the carcass of a male gazelle untouched and slowly decaying in the sun. He continued on after the scarab, the dusty dry land cracking below his feet, the occasional snap of twigs and desiccated lizards and mice kept him keenly aware of the extent of ruin this area encompassed. Then ahead, a standing pile of reddish boulders in the shade of which sat an old grey haired man. The scarab landed on his outstretched palm and he stared smiling with opaque blinded eyes as Aquilla approached.

"It is the right time for you to arrive."

Aquilla mulled this statement, hoping for more clarification.

"Why have I come?"

The old man laughed, pleased with this question. "You have come to learn all there is to learn before I am no more." He stood up shakily and walked over to Aquilla with his hand outstretched. Aquilla put his hand forward to touch his and the scarab walked into his hand and settled itself back down to its normal state of immobility. "The spirit being in your hand is over 10,000 years old. It was the first to cross and it is the herald of all that come after."

"What came after?"

"Many many things have come after, but most have not survived. Only the first spirit being always remains to search a new home and begin another day. That is why it has chosen you, for you represent everything it desires in a superior vessel to seek out the work and long path ahead."

"Exactly what traits do I hold in such rarity?"

"Your fire, your passion, your lack of fear. The pursuit you maintain for the most powerful experiences this world might offer you. You are a great mountain among men, chosen for your youth, your agility and your mind."

"Who has done this choosing? The beetle?"

"No no, the beetle has been dead for 10,000 years. It is the spirit being that inhabits the form of the beetle that calls out to you."

"And what does the spirit offer me for following its wishes?"

"Power, glory, overpowering ecstasy, passions unequalled in your experience. There is no power on Earth to compare to what you are being offered. It is a chance to be a god."

Abrafo was the old man's name. His age looked unimaginable. He wore rags that appeared to have been attached to him for years without replacement or cleaning. How he survived in this desolation on his own was a mystery unless he simply fed on the fresh dead animals that fell prey to the toxic land daily.

Aquilla was intrigued enough with the mystical elder to spend some time here learning what he could teach. He was never one to shy away from a challenge or adventure. They began with a sacrament. Abrafo lit fires in a circle around Aquilla placing him beside two stones uncovered by dusting the soil. The smoke had a peculiar flavor that enticed him. Then taking a curved blade, Abrafo gashed Aquilla across each breast, twice on his back, twice on his gut and once on each leg. He then took a grey paste and pressed it into each of these gashes. The paste burned and soon made him feel dizzy. Abrafo then presented him with a bowl of thick black mire and bade him to drink it whole. It tasted foul and he had to force his way through it. The effect was transfiguring. Over the course of a day and a half he saw visions and experiences that he could not explain or name. Violence and brutality in luscious passionate proportions. Cruelty measured out for pleasure. Defilement of the innocent, indoctrination of the once innocent into lusts of the most carnal and hungry nature. Unsatisfiable urges for domination – domination of everything. This ritual was repeated several more times over the next three weeks, during which he ate and drank he knew not, for Abrafo watched over him and tended to his needs as he fought with his new feelings and these primal experiences.

As he recovered from the forth session, Abrafo brought forward a cart with a basket filled with Pied Crows, their characteristic white breast and shoulders apparent as they squawked and fought within the case. He rolled the cart over a smoldering scented fire he had lit earlier, draping a heavy cloth over the cart to smoke the birds into submission. He then drew out some elaborate metal blades and presented them to Aquilla. "These blades are designed for such birds. You will start with the best bird we have and place him on the Earning Stone." He pointed to the left-most of the two stones. "You will place the remaining birds one at a time on the Giving Stone." Again he pointed, this time to the right-most stone.

Abrafo pulled the cover from the cart and the crows were panting on their sides at the bottom. He lifted the lid and search among them for the perfect specimen which he then handed to Aquilla. He found a short twig from the ground and daubed it within the thick black tonic he had fed Aquilla the last few weeks. He shoved this down the bird's throat, pushing it to swallow it. "Place this bird on the Earning Stone now." Aquilla did so and Abrafo followed him and selected one of the blades he had displayed earlier. He pointed at the bird's chest. "Here is its heart. You need to feel it, place your hand on it and be aware of it. You must pierce the chest of the bird so the five-pronged blade of this knife surrounds the heart. Press it deep down and into the stone. The stone will give way to the blade." Aquilla felt the solidity of the stone and could not see how the blades would do anything but bend upon impact with it. He looked at Abrafo once more to ascertain if this was sun madness or something miraculous. He pierced the bird. It flailed momentarily, fighting and opening its mouth to call, but was unable to do so. Shortly, it settled down, not dead yet, but surely on its way. Aquilla released the blade and found it had indeed sunk within the stone. In reaction, the stone was now giving off a glow of its own light. It no longer felt like stone, it felt like nothing he had experience or words to describe. He found it taking his breath away. "Good, now we must continue with the remaining birds."

They took each of the remaining seventeen birds one at a time to the Giving Stone and pierced them similarly through the chest until they were dead. The blade slid easily into this rock as well, and the two stones shared a rising glow as the ceremony progressed. Blood pooled and dripped from the Giving rock as they worked through to the tenth bird. By now, the first bird no longer struggled and had died as the rest. He continued the carnage through the last seven birds and stared at the lake of blood streaming from the rock below the final crow, his own hands dripping with it. He turned to Abrafo for direction. Abrafo simply smiled. The stones were glowing with a bright light by now, their touch was enticing, almost erotic. "Remove the blade from the bird." Abrafo instructed. "It is time to release it from our hold."

Aquilla pulled the blade out of the first bird and was awestruck when its leg twitched. The leg then slowly curled back to its chest and it grew still again. No movement on its chest, no movement at all. Then with a start, its wings spread out beneath it and both legs shot up as it struggled and righted itself on the stone. It stared at him from the stone and he stared back dumbstruck to understand. "It will serve you all your days as your eyes, your spy, your first warning of danger."

"Is it alive?"

"It is neither alive or dead. It is simply at your command from now until the end of days. Nothing will sway or prevent it from its duties to you. And this is but the first. We shall surround you with protectors, watch guards, spies and thieves. These will be the source of your power, they will make you master of men.

Aquilla and Abrafo made more crows, ravens and small songbirds. They knew his mind, he had only think of what concerned him and they would usher forth. He could not directly communicate with them or know their thought if they had such things, but they watched and they alerted and he grew to understand the meaning in their actions.

Bolstered by the euphoria of this skill, Aquilla chose to go further. He ordered 36 hyenas be brought to him and spent a long dark bloody night of endless slaughter to create two of his most ferocious familiars – Eshe and Lazarus. But he did not stop there, paying an outrageous sum for 18 lioness he summoned his most feared monster – Bast the undefeatable. Surely a work of unmatched glory, Bast the beautiful. Bast the deadly. Bast the merciless.

As Aquilla receives word that his dynasty in Cape Coast was in jeopardy from new competition and changing tides, he choose one final act of creation – that of Mephisto the spider monkey. Abrafo warned that monkeys are unlike other familiars and sometimes showcase a mind of their own. This was of no concern to Aquilla once he saw his creation rise up from the dead. He saw in its eyes the cunning he required for the challenges ahead.

Aquilla gathered the stones onto a wagon and made preparations to return to Cape Coast. The birds flew ahead to scout and learn the new realities. Abrafo said he could not accompany him. His energy was spent in awaiting for Aquilla's arrival and he could feel the salt falling from him already.

It took no time at all for Aquilla to reclaim his dominance in Cape Coast. His emissaries identified his enemies far before he reached the city. Returning by nightfall, he ushered Eshe, Lazarus and Bast on a night-long murder spree. By morning there was nothing left of those that threatened him. Entire networks had been slaughtered top to bottom. They were all savaged by animals – demons that came in the night it was claimed. The carnage was unthinkable and widespread throughout the city and nearby country. The military, police and quickly assembled militias spread out looking for the man-slayers. It was assumed a pair of lions had attacked as a lion had been seen, but there were other reports, of two headed lions, dogs bathed in fire, a giant snakes with the face of a man. The dread was widespread and did not fade with the fact that the murderous night was not repeated. It was made worse that these demons were never found and never seen again. Surely they were just waiting for their next opportunity.

Aquilla commanded Cape Coast for another five years. He built a private villa in which he placed the stones and held lavish orgies with dozens of women all succumbing to the dark potion that lit fires within your soul and drove your mind to madness. They fucked endlessly upon the stones mixing sweat, cum and blood in extravagant patterns of pain and pleasure. He grew more ruthless in his punishment of his partners seeking a painful passioned union that he felt somehow would bring him peace. Many of those attending these sybarite affairs became initiates of the cult, drawn in by the ever increasing lustful agony the carnal acts and drugs on the stones brought them. Nothing compared in its desire and compulsion. Nothing else in their life made them feel important and part of something larger than everything else around them. Mephisto and the crows kept eye on those that did not choose to take part. Inevitably some foul tragedy would befall these souls for this poor judgement. Since the monkey drew far less attention than the hyenas or Bast, Mephisto became the prime assassin of Aquilla's enemies. The beast showed intelligence and decision making that was not present in the other familiars. Mephisto became adept at the use of poisons, applying them to his victims as they slept or mixing them into their food and drink.

After five years, Aquilla felt the desire for change. With all this time having past, he finally let his mind return to his father. He wanted to show the old picaroon what he had made of himself. Perhaps he might like to watch Obediah slowly die in the most gruesome way he could find fitting. He prepared to sail back to America bringing his wealth, his followers, the demons he had conjured and the stones – of course the stones.

It was with the greatest of pomp and circumstance that Aquilla made his way back into Milledgeville. His wagon train was peculiar, massive and hinted at exotic riches. The glare of dark eyes through cages colored the imaginations of children running alongside it. Little could they surmise their wildest dreams dare not compare to the reality of those cold eyes. His flock flew ahead and landed scouts amidst the trees of the plantation. Souza was the first to notice this, for the Pied Crow was indigenous to her homeland and she remembered their white chests well.

She rushed inside to tell Obediah that guests were arriving, though the wagons were still some way off and too far for her to see.

Obediah dressed himself in his best, uncertain whom he was preparing to greet. He made his way down the stairs and out the front door as the wagons began to draw their way up his road. Everyone came out to see what was happening as they'd never seen such a parade. The lead wagon came to a halt just before Obediah and there was silence for a moment as the driver looked on, but no movement came from inside.

Consternated by this delay, Obediah walked over to the door of the wagon intent on swinging it open, when Aquilla stepped forward and eyed him sharply from above. He lingered on the stairs of the wagon to retain his height. He had grown tall since his father had seen him, but his father would always be the taller man.

"Father." He said stepping down and facing the old man straight on. Obediah looked on dumbstruck, unable to formulate a thought. "I've brought you a fresh horse to make up for the one I stole when I left. I also have replacements for mother's jewels and the tools I took on my departure." A man brought the horse in question around to Obediah and two other men bore a chest which they placed at his feet and opened up to reveal its contents. "I trust mother and yourself have been well during my absence."

With this Obediah found his voice. "She's dead."

There was quiet for a moment as this was subsumed. "Well, I suppose that is to be expected. It would have happened had I remained or not I'm certain."

"Why are you back?" Obediah spat, his breath growing gravelly and erratic.

"Why?" Aquilla answered stepping closer to him. "Why, what really could be more obvious? I'm here to give my thanks to the father that provided me the opportunity to succeed as I have in my life. And I have succeeded remarkably well Obediah." He purposely used his father's name, something he had never dared to do as a child.

"You can't stay, I won't have it!"

"Ah, let's concern ourselves with the details of accommodations later. What is more important now is to familiarize myself with all that has transpired here in the last nine years."

"What has transpired is none of your concern as upon your leaving you ceased to be a part of this family. You are not wanted here and I will not stand for you —" It was at this point that Eshe and Lazarus approached, having been released from their cage. They stared at Obediah unleashing their maniacal laughter as he stepped back in bafflement.

"No need for standing father. Souza, lets arrange a fine dinner party. I brought lots of goods from town and the finest of chefs. This is going to be a homecoming to remember!"

Obediah found himself a prisoner in his own home with the return of Aquilla. He wasn't prevented from leaving, but everywhere he went there were eyes. The people that came back with Aquilla and those queer crows that always seemed to be somewhere. No one, not even Souza seemed to be on his side against Aquilla. They all were elated at his return and the gifts he brought. He brooded to himself, drinking his port alone in his study wishing it all away. Staring at his photo of his beloved Francine.

Aquilla took over run of the plantation adding buildings for the cult followers he brought with him. He hid the stones carefully and kept Bast out of sight in a crypt he'd built under the house. Mephisto and the hyenas were allowed to run free, he just wanted Bast in case of an emergency and preferred she be unknown.

Souza approached him. "Sir, it is such a pleasure to have you back with us. We've awaited your return with utmost excitement."

"I missed you too Souza, you always kept a special place in my heart even when I was far away."

"These places you visited, they were home to me before I was brought here."

"You are from Cape Coast?"

"No, I am from Cameroon." She smiled as she said this and he got her point.

"Abrafo wasn't the only survivor was he?"

"No sir, he was not."

"How many of you?"

"Four of us ended up here with your family."

"And what, this was fate? That you should find your way to the very plantation where I am to be born and set out on this — odyssey to recover your artifacts?"

"We saw it as your destiny, even before you were born. The stars told us of your coming. Your strength, your courage. We knew you were our hope the moment you were conceived."

This information threw Aquilla nearly into a rage. Manipulation of his life by his own house slaves no less! "What of Clarissa? Did you drive her away so that I might engage this madness for you?" He grabbed her by the throat and lifted her from the ground shaking in his anger.

"It was Obediah. He sent her away. She was with his child."

Aquilla dropped Souza and nearly lost his balance, grabbing the table harshly and knocking over a bowl and several glasses to shatter on the floor. He would kill him, not quickly, but slowly he would kill that damnation of a man.

Jacob pounded down the hill as fast as his feet could carry him, panting heavily and holding his arms before him to block the slapping branches in his way. The mother brown bear refused to give up her chase of him and he felt surely he would die from lack of breath before she even got her paws on him. He climbed the next rise and ran down and through the stream below, finally spotting signs of humanity up ahead of him. He burst through the forest into a small garden and collided immediately with Idalia. Idalia dropped the carrots and tomatoes she was carrying with a squeal and Jacob tumbled face first into the cabbages. He spun back up and looked for the bear, but it was nowhere to be seen. He had raced right through the open back gate and plowed directly into the daughter of the household.

She stared at him dumbfound and he was at a loss to explain. "I'm sorry. Truly I'm sorry! I'll pay for everything, I can work for your pa. It was a bear, she was chasing me in the woods, I thought I was done for."

Idalia started laughing wildly, she fell back in the dirt and just let herself laugh, for she was kind and laughter came easily to her. She was ten, the same age as Jacob. She had long straight blonde hair that she pulled back in two pony tails as she worked amidst the vegetables. "Why was the bear after you?"

"I was in the woods hunting squirrels with my slingshot when I saw a bear cub in front of me. By then it was too late, the mama bear was charging me and I didn't have no time to think."

"Do you always bother mother bears? Surely they taught you that's a bad idea."

"I know enough of about bears, that cub just snuck up on me is all. I'm good in the woods, I know my way around better than anyone. This just was a remarkable circumstance I found myself in."

"Idalia, what's going on out here?" Idalia father Bartholomew came out of the house to the garden. "Boy, what is the meaning of this!? Why are you ransacking my garden?"

"Its a remarkable circumstance daddy." Idalia giggled in response.

Jacob turned between Idalia and her father, scared, confused, but unable to not laugh at her contagious joy. Soon all three were laughing heartily with the father not knowing what was funny but caught in the mood of the moment. "What's your name son?"

"Jacob sir."

"Well Jacob, why don't you come in and introduce yourself and give us the story behind this remarkable circumstance."

It was late at night, less than a week after Aquilla confronted Souza, that Mephisto entered Obediah's room as he lay sleeping. The monkey silently crept over the great man's bed with a dropper in its left hand. Climbing carefully upon the headboard and wrapping its tale about a post for support, Mephisto leaned gently over Obediah's head and ever so delicately lifted his right eyelid to trickle two droplets and then let it close. He did the same with the left eye and then, satisfied, scampered silently back out of the room.

In the morning Obediah cried out in terror calling for Souza. Souza rushed to the room and, after fevered screams and words, came out and called for someone to fetch the doctor.

The diagnosis was grim. The doctor could not give an explanation, but Obediah had lost sight in both of his eyes overnight. The eyes were white and calloused. Completely opaque, not a spark of light would ever find their way through again.

"Its witchcraft!" Obediah shouted. "They've done this to me!" He began to cry, the full impact of his pitiful situation growing ever more real for him. "Damn you all! Damn you! Damn you!" He lashed out with anything his hands fell upon, his water pitcher, his bed shoes, his pillows until he fell to the ground weeping in despair.

Jacob and Idalia became fast friends from their first encounter. She shared his enthusiasm for the wilderness and he tolerated he interest in flowers and gardening. They spend more time together than they did with their other friends and grew to have their own inside jokes and pranks during school.

Jacob would build tree houses and find caves to explore and he'd invite her to join him. He was strong, adventurous and never found time to be bored. She loved his short cut brown hair and brown eyes. He was always wearing out his clothes and shoes from rocks, briars and raspberry bushes. She'd never seen him with a clean shirt or pair of pants and there was always a hole in them somewhere. They'd make campfires and cook crawdads and squirrels he'd catch. Eventually Jacob caught wind of some extraordinary beasts at the Stafford plantation and talked Idalia into sneaking over to take a look.

"What kind of animals are they?"

"Dunno, its not a dog though. Its bigger and meaner than that they say."

"Maybe something from far away, like from Africa. Maybe it's a lion."

"No I don't think it's a cat, its easy to tell a cat no matter how big it might be, still looks like a cat. I'm betting its some kind of wild beast he's brought back from India or China. Maybe something that has wings even."

"Wings? On a dog?"

"In China, they got wings on all kinds of things. I've seen pictures."

"Yeah well I'll believe that when I see it myself."

They crept through the forest behind the property, stopping briefly to explore when they found the cave Clarissa had stayed in to recover from her assault by Obediah. They past the wood shed and came to the edge of Stafford Plantation. The stream was in front of them and they naturally went to explore it. The water was fresh and sweet. Jacob started hunting under the rocks for crawdads and Idalia sat upon the fallen tree singing 'Three Crows' as she noticed the unusual white breasted crows looking down on them from above.

"Find me something to put these crawdads in. There's a bunch of them in here."

Idalia tread carefully off the log watching her step and then stood face to face with Lazarus. She screamed and ran into the stream to hold onto Jacob. Jacob's eyes grew wide at the sight of the massive beast. A sinister laughter issued from the other side of the stream and they both turned to she Eshe watching them as well. The two beasts sat on either shore watching the children as the sun set. Standing in the stream they began to get chill and shivered holding each other closely, Jacob asking Idalia to stop crying but she couldn't help it.

"Why did we come here Jacob?"

"Its my fault, I'll get us out of this." He spied a figure walking towards them in the growing dark. He shouted out, "Help! We got lost and these animals have us trapped in the water! You've got to help us please!"

Aquilla walked up and stood beside Lazarus surmising the situation quickly and laughed. "What are your names?"

"I'm Jacob and this is Idalia, we just got lost is all."

"You look cold Idalia. How long have you been standing in the water?"

"I don't know." She babbled, unable to stop shivering or crying.

Aquilla waded into the water and lifted her in his arms. "Let's get you two warmed up before we send you back home. I'm sure your parents would appreciate us bringing you back dry and fed.

Jacob followed Aquilla back to the manor with the hyenas following them on either side. "What are these, some kind of dogs?"

Aquilla laughed again. He enjoyed the bravery of Jacob. "They are hyenas Jacob. From Africa. They like to eat carrion and prey on the weak, which is perhaps why they took such an interest in you two."

"Would they have eaten us?" Asked Idalia.

"No sweetheart, they wouldn't eat you I can promise you that."

Jacob and Idalia were invited to come to the plantation whenever they pleased after that evening. Aquilla took Jacob under his wing and taught him true hunting with a rifle and with a bow. They spent a great amount of time together in the wilderness and Aquilla looked upon him much as a son.

Aquilla's lust for adventure pressed him once again to travel. He first made his way up the east coast to New York where he established a drug and prostitution empire similar to his rein on Cape Coast. It was exciting and challenging, with much bigger threats against him. He reveled in the challenge, taking only his crows and Mephisto with him to test his own guile and appetite for danger. His strength and fearlessness drew men and women alike to him and he never encountered failure regardless how aggressively his rivals approached him. There was no place safe enough to keep Mephisto out. Politicians, police officials, crime lords, they all fell prey to unexplained deaths in the night, while out to dinner or in the midst of a crowded party. With time, Aquilla became bored of New York and moved west, stopping first in Chicago to reiterate his dominance of all foes of any flavor.

He then pressed on to California where he explored and conquered from Mexico into Alaska, intoxicated by the adventure, suspense of new foes, and the ever new pleasures of women, drugs and pain — sensational levels of shared erotic pain. California had everything he craved to indulge his burning passions. He lapped heavily of its riches and felt the growing pangs of desire for something even greater. Something pleasurable in world-shattering proportions.

The years past and the war began. Jacob was called up to service. He'd grown into a strong handsome young man and her beauty defied explanation to him. She let her hair fall down these days below her hat as she worked in the garden. The warm glow of the sun playing amidst the cascade of it was the very face of God to him. Idalia wept uncontrollably on the day he was taken from her. She swore to pray for him every day and he promised he would return to her the minute they won. She spent her days working in the family garden and in other gardens growing food for the troops. At night she sewed uniforms. Her family had to give up the majority of their crops as the war wound on and they found themselves growing hungry. In desperation Idalia went up to Stafford Plantation to seek Aquilla for help. Stafford had been spared the burden of the war. No one knew quite why, but it was guessed either through bribery or fear of the monsters that lurked in that place. With Aquilla out west, Souze said Idalia could stay at the plantation and work any of the fields she chose for her own family, especially her mother who had grown frail that year. She wrote Jacob regularly and he always sent word back to her that he was safe and desperate to see her again. But the Battle of Atlanta was on hand, and the turn of the war was a desperate one. She feared as Jacob headed to support the troops already in Atlanta.

Word then came to Aquilla that Clarissa had been spotted in Atlanta. She had been freed from the house she served and was now with Union troops. To finally hear word of her after all this time, he had expected it would have no impact upon him. But he burned inside with a frenzy. He rushed back east as fast as he was able. He took thirteen of his own horses and stole four more from neighboring farms and for the first time since coming back to America he positioned the stones and began a ceremony. Souze and the other cult members helped. They performed it deep in the woods away from the others, but the sounds of dying horses carried throughout the valley. Terrifying frantic cries that went on and on through the night. A lake of blood flowed from the stones into the crystal stream, darkening it in a way that it was never said to recover. In the morning, Aquilla sat atop Balthazar, his demon war horse. He rode to Atlanta, his hyenas beside him and the crows spotting out ahead. Anyone they passed on the road gave way and looked in horror at the stern rider, the crazed beasts and the ghost horse that seemed never to tire. They charged on endlessly without rest until they neared Atlanta. The crows had found the barracks she was being kept in the south of the city. They had to pass Confederate troops first and were provided the best route to avoid them, the hyenas dispatching anyone that remained in their way. Soon they crossed into Union-held Atlanta and used the same strategy to slide their way towards the barracks holding Clarissa. Dispatching the guards placed before it, Aquilla rode his horse within, startlingly everyone into a panic of screams and frantic running. The crows landed beside Clarissa and she turned to flee only to face Lazarus at her side. Aquilla approached her on Balthazar and without explanation swung her in his arms onto the back of the great horse and, leaping back himself, they charged out. She screamed, uncertain who he was or what was happening. The uproar had drawn attention and Union troops had rushed to the scene. The hyenas did their work, but one shot struck Aquilla in the shoulder as he road Balthazar hard and fast out of town. The alarm had been called and troops came from everywhere. Gunfire rained out against him and he did his best to use the cover of darkness and the swiftness of his steed to outdistance his enemies. The hyenas sprinted ahead to prepare a path through Confederate lines whom has also been alerted to the mayhem. Shots ran out from both sides and Aquilla was struck once more in the leg. He did not know this bullet hit Clarissa as well and she struggled to remain conscious from the pain. They drove hard on through Confederate lines and back towards Milledgeville.

The plantation was a boil of activity when Aquilla returned with the fading Clarissa. Both of their wounds were dressed and Aquilla refused to leave Clarissa's side until she regained herself. Souza finally convinced him to get his own rest and he collapsed immediately in exhaustion. Clarissa was left alone. She had been pretending to be unconscious until she was left to herself. She now sat up heavily and found Obediah standing at the door before her. His white calloused eyes stared blankly ahead as he listened for her movement and a gruesome little smile crossed his chapped lips as he heard her bed creak. His face was unshaven with several weeks of scraggled growth. His hair unkept and the clothing he wore appeared to have stayed on him for some time, stained with dropped food and urine across the front. The scent of him crossed the room to her, the smell of old piss and aged man stink. "I heard you were back. How nice of you to join us at the end."

She stared at him as he stood between her and the exit she had been waiting for.

"It is the end you know. The Yankees are on their way here now from Atlanta. They'll burn this place to the ground and me with it God-willing. I can smell death in the air. It's refreshing. More poetic an odor since my dearest Francine –" Clarissa, stepped painfully from the bed and pushed passed him, knocking

Obediah into a table and down to the floor. The China kettle from the table struck his head and broke apart leaving a gash that bled across his ruined left eye.

Clarissa stumbled painfully towards the front door but was intercepted by Souza grabbing her and worked to calm her down. "Easy now! You're safe dear. Easy!"

Clarissa broke out in deep sobs, "Please let me go, please! I need to find my son! He's still in Atlanta. I need my baby!" Clarissa sank in Souza's arms to the floor wailing and crying for her child. Aquilla and the house staff ran to see the commotion. Obediah was found bleeding, cackling madly on the floor and was escorted back to his room. They wrestled Clarissa back to bed. "Please let me go find my son. I can't live without him."

"Where is your boy?" Souza asked her.

"He was with me when you took me. They kept the boys in another room. I don't know where he is now but I need to find him. He's all I got in the world!"

Aquilla's world spun with this news. He had dreamed Clarissa would be overjoyed to see him, but she refused to even look him in the eye. Her heart was set on the bastard son of his lecherous father Obediah. So be it. He would find the child and bring him back to her. He could not blame the boy for Obediah's depravity.

"What is the boy's name Clarissa?" Asked Souza still trying to calm her.

"Samuel."

The crows were issued forth immediately in the search.

Aquilla once again charged the path back to Atlanta. By now Union troops where heading this way and he passed Confederate soldiers fleeing the battle to protect their families. The crows led him and the hyenas through the safest course, but this time he brought Bast with him as well. The three beasts plowed a ruinous path through soldiers from either side, even civilians that got in the way of their mad flight for Samuel. They reached the barracks once more and Aquilla stood back on Balthazar as Eshe, Lazarus and Bast lay waste to countless Union jackets in a wide circle around the building, not willing to risk any more wounds to befall Aquilla. Eventually Aquilla rode Balthazar back into the building for a second time and he followed the crows to the boy Samuel, who stood wide-eyed with other young children against the wall. He stepped from the horse and lifted the boy on the back of the saddle and they left once again to return him to his beloved mother Clarissa.

During the ride back through the night Samuel became brave enough to ask questions.

"Are those lions?"

Aquilla felt a surprising calming at the sound of the boy's voice. He had been fighting his natural inclination to despise him as the offshoot of all evil.

"Bast is, yes. The other two are Eshe and Lazarus. They are hyenas from Africa."

"They are bigger than any dog I've ever seen."

"They are bigger and stronger than anything you've ever seen I promise you that Samuel."

"Where are you taking me?"

"Back to your mother, she is worried about you."

With this Samuel grew silent and in awe. He felt he was in some sort of dream.

The miles wound on as they made great speed towards Milledgeville. Clarissa had no knowledge or hope of this. She was desperate to get back to her child. She had finally got him safely in Union hands with her and had praised God for her great fortune. The cruel joke that was now played on her, finding herself without Samuel back in this accursed place where all her life's misery began, she blamed the devil himself for this trickery. When Obediah appeared with his glassy white eyes stinking of death, she felt that Satan had come to laugh at her from his having snatched her from the very seat of heaven. She fought with the window of her room and drew it open. Climbing out and dropping to the grass below, she ran off down the road. Desperate for any help that might aid her in getting back to her son in Atlanta. Surely the Union troops where getting close. If she could only find them, she would have her passage back to her son.

Souze watched from another window as Clarissa ran across the fields to leave the plantation. She walked outside and back to behind the house to where Abraham was tending the horses. "Its time, get the wagon."

Abraham, Socrates, Lilian and Souze headed down the road in pursuit of Clarissa. They caught up with her walking her way to Atlanta and she ran from the road into the forest. They pulled the wagon over and dashed after her. Her leg was still terribly injured and she moaned from the pain as she struggled to distance herself from her pursuers. Socrates caught her by the hair and wrapped his arm around her neck choking her. She kicked out and Abraham grabbed her legs and they held her against the ground. He tore the clothes off of her and beat her with a thick stick across the stomach and legs. He then dropped his trousers and forced himself upon her, tearing her vagina roughly from the violence. He spit down into her to moisten the passage and continued to fuck her until he was satisfied. Trading places with Abraham, the process continued until both men had their fill of her and their semen and her blood poured warmly out upon the dried leaves and red clay. They lifted her up and beat her across the face and slashed her across the chest with the same stick until it broke, at which time Abraham simply kicked at her back until she was struggling to breath. Souza approached and wrapped a rope around Clarissa's neck and pulled it tight. She could barely struggle at this point, her eyes bulging out and her face growing fat and dark with the pressure of blood. Finally her tongue swelled through her lips and she was no more.

They bore Clarissa's body back to her bed, wailing and crying about their loss. Everyone was in dismay and word quickly spread it was the Union troops who were at the outskirts of town preparing the invasion. Panic ensued, many people fleeing town, others robbing from those who had already left, some bolting themselves in their homes for an inevitable showdown, still others went to hide in the caves in the nearby woods.

Idaliah ushered her parents to follow her to the Stafford Plantation. She felt Aquilla was the only one that could protect them. At long last, her parents agreed and they set off to the great manor. They were greeted by the wailing of grief for Clarissa and Idalia did her best to console Dapney, Clarissa's grandmother. By now gunfire could be heard in the distance as the battle lines drew near. Everyone filed into the mansion uncertain what to do next or what fate was about to deal them.

Jacob, fleeing a front line that was futile to try to hold, ran back amidst shots from his own men as a deserter. His skills in the forest served him well and he eluded those hunting him, making his way through the back woods to Idaliah's home. She was not there, having already left for Stafford. He saw no evidence of struggle or theft, for their house was poor and the food had already been taken long ago. He guessed her location and made his way carefully in the dark back to the plantation. Lead Union troops were already on the streets of Milledgeville and he kept himself out of their sight. Childhood spent sneaking at night helped him avoid any dogs that would bark upon seeing him. He worked his way to the back entrance of the plantation where years before Idalia and he had been caught in the stream by Eshe and Lazarus. As he approached, men pointed guns at him and one fired, but he waved his Confederate cap and kept his hands in the air calling out he meant no harm. They led him back to the manor and as they approached Abraham and Socrates returned in the wagon filled with men dressed in the Central State Hospital gowns. Jacob ran into the house and called out for Idaliah. She heard his voice and felt a rush of emotion through her body. "Jacob!" She called, tears already running down her face. "Jacob!" And then they saw each other. Not allowing a second to pass, they ran into each other's arms and he swung her about him clutching her tightly, tears running warmly down their cheeks as they smothered each other with kisses over every inch of their faces, finally he lingered on the sweet lips he'd dreamed of every day and every night on the battlefield. "It's really you, I can't believe it!"

"Neither can I. When I heard they were about to take Milledgeville I ran as fast as I could to be here with you."

"I love you Jacob."

"Oh Idaliah, every moment I breath belongs to you. You own me in more ways than can be counted."

Aquilla stood suddenly at the doorway, in his hand he held the hand of Samuel. Souza came, tears running down her face to stop him from going any further. "You don't want to go in there."

"Get away from me." He pushed passed her having seen the emotion on the faces outside and knowing they could have but one cause. He entered her room. The white sheet they'd cast over her had blood soaked at her face, stomach and legs. He ripped the sheet off, not thinking that the boy was still held in his hand. He stared at the desecration that had been weighed upon her. The butchery of the thing he loved most in the world. Samuel stared, unable to speak or even think. He could not recognize his mother for her face had been so deformed, she looked only as a despicable joke of his true mother's beauty.

"How?" Was all Aquilla could breath out to say.

Souza took the boy from his hand and sheltered his face into her dress, she then passed him on to Lilian to take him from the miserable room. "She ran to find her son and the Union soldiers found her before we did."

He breathed this information in, never taking his eyes off her contorted face, lost of all beauty it once had in such abundance. He touched her shoulder, one of the few areas he could still recognize as her. She was still warm, but coolness was settling upon her.

"I want them to pay."

Souza vibrated at this statement, the culmination of her work finally within view. "You know what needs to be done. Abrafo told you your destiny, its been your choice as to when to take it."

He turned to her not quite understanding her meaning but sensing it nonetheless.

"Its time for you to become the god you were meant to be. Purge this world of its madness and cruelty. It's your right to rule above any president or king, you have only to take it."

Shots rang out in the back fields of the plantation and it was clear the Union troops were arriving. Aquilla issued forward his warrior familiars to dispatch them and watched from the roof of the manor as they cut down men like blades of grass, suffering no wounds though they were each shot and stabbed repeatedly over the years. He felt his own wounded shoulder, contemplated his own place in such a world. A god among men. All knowing, all powerful not suffering to the opinions of these states or those, this nation or that. An ageless rule with no need of an heir, no weakening monarch failing in his old age. He watched a soldier ripped down and split open by Bast, his head bursting from his body to fly across the field from her overwhelming force. He decided to become a god.

They brought the stones out and placed them in the open field behind the barn. Torches were lit with the exotic oils and he breathed them in to remember their familiar smell. Souza brought forward white tunics for the cult members to wear as well as one for Aquilla. They also brought tunics for the lunatics that Abraham had brought from the hospital. She drank from a goblet and then filled it once more to present to him. He drank it hungrily and threw it from him, lifting her in his strong arms forcing her down upon his erection. He slapped her and screamed at her words of hatred and malice, punishing her for all the wrongs that had befallen him. She took his punishment, craving it, luxuriating in the mixture of brutality and intense pleasure. He bit into her nipple drawing blood and she cried from it. He held her down by her neck and lifted her leg to plunge deeper inside her as she clawed at his arm for breath.

Meanwhile the ceremony continued around him and Bast, Eshe and Lazarus kept the soldiers at bay. The Union was made aware of their unexpected losses at the plantation and drew up plans for a full assault. Several of the lunatics managed to escape during the mayhem leaving only thirteen. Canon fire began to rain down onto the fields from afar. Souza and Abraham lay Aquilla down upon the Earning stone. Souza was now naked, dripping blood from her left breast and covered in sweat. She lifted a massive forked blade above Aquilla and with the fire of anticipation in her eyes drove it through his chest. He felt no pain, only disconnection. The world around him became fogged and muted. He felt a pulse from the stone below him, the sensation of fingers touching, feeling, experiencing him from beyond.

He watched as the first of the lunatics were led to the second stone and slaughtered. One after another they went below Souza's blade. Her deliberation was irrepressible. He felt the strength of these falling souls course through him, pounding into his heart. On and on it went, and he smiled knowing this was right, his destiny had always led to this. At once they ran out of lunatics. For a moment their was concern, but Souza made a decision and they dawned new robes and rushed to the house. Aquilla was in a mid-experience of reality. No longer part of that which surrounded him, but not fully apart from it. He felt his body changing, he felt the strength of aeons of knowledge coursing into him. They brought his father next and he watched the ghastly swine fall down on his blind face against the glowing stone and laughed inside to watch blood flowing from his mouth as she stabbed him threw from behind. Another wave of knowledge and understanding filled him. His body tingled and he heard voices – chanting, howling voices. Voices crossing unimaginable voids of time and distance to come to his ears. Then he saw Samuel being brought next to the stone and he felt a pause in his thought. He looked from the corpse of his abhorrent father and the face of the boy before him and suddenly he knew — knew for sure this was not his father's bastard, it was his own son. His heart began to race and the boy looked into his eyes. His eyes, drunk with the poison Souza had given to all of them, they drooped and could not properly focus, yet even so he saw his own likeness. He saw his own blood.

He fought to move his arm, withdraw the blade from him. The effort was immense, he felt the stone itself holding him down. He tried to call out to Souza to stop, don't use the boy! But his voice was no longer his own. He was frozen within his fading body unable to do anything but watch as his only son, the beloved child of the true love of his life was pressed down against the stone and stabbed through the heart. He saw the blood, the life flow from Samuel. A tear streamed down his face as he began to regret his every life decision that had culminated in this madness. It was over, Samuel was dead. Socrates pulled his bleeding corpse from the rock and led Jacob towards it next. Jacob, whom he'd viewed as the son he'd never had. Why must so much be given up for what? Simply for him? He wasn't seeking justice for Clarissa in this way, he was seeking eternal rule for himself.

Another cannonball strike, this one beside the stones, bodies went flying. Aquilla felt his soul leaving his body and from above the trees he watched himself solitary on the stone. Souza, Abraham, Jacob and Idalia and the others were sprawled across the grass as the smoke from the strike billowed across them. Union troops flooded the area firing at anyone who fled and capturing those that gave up. He floated further away as more of the soldiers entered the plantation, charging through the house, gathering everyone they could out in the field, staring aghast at the pile of fifteen corpses beside the single corpse of Aquilla. What madness they must have thought. What depravity had driven these people to such an action?

Aquilla floated further above. He saw his crows all fallen to the earth. He could not see Bast or the hyenas but he expected the same had befallen them. This was the true fate he'd earned, not that of a god, but of a merciless madman who'd taken countless lives with him on his descent into hell.

Part II
There is no Out

My father was an uncommon man. Self made, rich beyond dreams, easily bored, always seeking new adventures. He was a happy man, hard working, devoted to his family. He needed to be first. He needed to push himself beyond any boundaries he felt constraining him. He was never the tallest and made up for it with cunning, fearlessness and hard work. It was to this end, as the Soviet Union began to crumble, he agitated with interest. He researched Russia, studied the language and prepared to travel there seeking fortune and excitement. "It's the wild west!" He'd tell me, "In my own lifetime, how can that be passed up?"

My mother and I worried about him when he'd go. He'd stay weeks at a time, and eventually months, as he strove to find opportunity and unique experiences. He started buying and opening factories in towns across Russia promising real jobs and opportunities to people confused and frightened by the new world cast upon them. He came back to us after starting his fourth such factory, filled with success and exhilaration. He lavished us with an unusual collection of exotic gifts that he'd collected on the way. For me, it was an amazing intricate hand-made wooden boat inside a bottle. It was so small and so fragile I could have balanced it on the end of my finger. I marveled endlessly at its craftsmanship and the care that went into such delicate work. For my mother he brought a dazzling necklace of Russian red gold and Russian diamonds. She flushed as he put it around her neck and I left the room to give them privacy. I was preparing for school at Harvard having just finished high school. The world seemed completely open to me and I had not yet chosen to make a decision of what path I wished to take. I had faith, the world would point me in a direction shortly if I just kept my eyes and mind open to possibilities.

The wait did not prove to be long at all. One of the treasures my father had brought back for himself was a very eccentric old silver blade with five sharp ends that made a sort of circular opening in the midst of them. It was as peculiar and it was disconcerting. It left me uncomfortable when I held it as he first showed it to me. Accompanying the odd blade he had purchased a box of some oddly off-smelling incense and a small bottle of a dark liquid he claimed was a powerful old elixir with properties not even the seller was able to describe to him. The smell from this was exceptionally pungent. I felt uneasy after sniffing it and put it down immediately. I excused myself from the room with a suddenly panicked increase in the beat of my heart. My father laughed as I receding. "I had the same reaction son!" He called after me as I left. "When you experience the dangerous and honest intensities of life, their glow can be intimidating. The secret is not to run, but embrace what at first feels beyond you."

I closed the door to my bedroom. I felt a rush of emotions. I felt sudden anger at my father, uncertain of its origin. I felt fear. And I felt exhilaration. I felt a deep anticipation that something tremendous, something world-altering was about to happen in my life and I would never be the same. I threw myself beneath my sheets and shivered though I was not cold. The dark felt both a comfort and a foreboding. I could not decide if I would rather dash up and turn on a light or bury myself deeper in my blankets. I chose not to move and sat shaking with wide eyes for some time before the feeling subsided and I fell into a nervous chaotic sleep. My dreams were of dark soundless forests with moss covered floors and silent canopies. Deep silence accompanied by furtive figures slipping quietly between trees around me. Suddenly, I saw a gowned woman far off from me, look directly at me before arms reached out from behind a tree and pulled her away. I ran to the spot she was, nothing to be seen but a darkness in the moss shining under the dim moonlight. Touching this darkness, warm wetness on my fingers in the pale light of the moon. It looked to be blood. I started to hear screams, screams mixed with agony and ecstasy from somewhere off seemingly before and then behind me. I was uncertain where to turn. I came upon a clear spring-fed lake whose pristine quality provided me to see within its depths even in this dim light. On the floor of the lake I could see naked bodies of young women, boys and girls lying with a peace of having travelled beyond the reach of pain. Their transition must have been deeply traumatic however, for their bodies showed signs of torture and their chests had a ring of wounds surrounding their hearts. One of these was the girl I had seen in the gown earlier. Her eyes seemed to be locked onto me from below the lightly rippling water. She had a peace on her face and I felt she was beckoning me towards her. I stepped into the chill springs and walked towards her. She reached her hand up for me with a smile on her face. I lifted her from below the waves and held her against me, her long dark hair draining the spring water behind her. She pulled towards me and kissed me generously on the lips, cold and lifeless but still filled with a love and a memory of life that made me cry for her tragedy. She whispered, "Find me, my love" She repeated this to me again and again as I held her and caressed her hair, tears trailing from my face.

"I will" I promised. "I will find you. What is your name?"

"Dafna" She answered and she placed a circular silver amulet on a chain in my hand. It had weight in it from the water of the spring lake that was dripping from it. The weight inside led me to feel there was something more within it, for the silver was delicately ornate, made as a sort of cage. What was within was impossible to tell in the dark, but the spring water continued to drip from it. She held me tighter. "They are coming now, use it against them." Through the forest streamed bats spinning and swirling about us. I swung the amulet erratically at them trying to strike one, but they evaded not just the sphere but the spray of water is issue from it. I began to swing it about me in a circular eight patter and it kept them at bay. Eventually I was simply swinging it in a circle and they kept a wide distance from me. In my arms Dafna began to let go and sink back down.

"Where will I find you Dafna?" I pleaded, still spilling the orb about my head.

"Follow Benjamin, follow the stones and following the path back to your home. It mustn't happen again."

I was awakened by the sound gunshots.

I sat motionless and without emotion. I could not feel my body. I could not sense time. I was unsure if I was breathing or my heart was beating.

Before me lay my mother, her eyes open, her body exposed, bruises and lacerations across her face, chest, legs and arms. Her neck was a deep purple and her probably downfall. Beside her on the bed still sitting upright, his head slumped forward, was my father. The revolver had fallen from his hand. His blood and brain matter patterned the ceiling above. He had deep scratches as well on his arms, his face, neck, chest and back. He had bite marks on his left cheek and around his right nipple. A burner with the incense he had brought back with him was slowly smoldering out beside the bed. It filled the room with an odor that confused me, left me anxious yet drawn to it. They each had drained glasses beside the bed, and the disturbing vial was uncorked, its elixir half depleted. I stared at this scene for an eternity, at least it was so in my mind. I knew my life had ended and a new one had begun. All my ambitions, plans and interest; their meaning abolished by this one new reality. Everything I had understood had just been turned on its head by forces that I did not understand but now saw as a threat that I would fight with my dying breath for the revenge I felt building ever so slowly within me. It was but a spark at the moment, overwhelmed by shock and loss as it was in the immediate. But there as a strength and patience in this spark. It would not be denied. It would not falter in its pursuit regardless of the pressures and agencies fanned out against it.

I held a small rag in my hand and carefully dumped the remaining incense from the box into another container I brought. I then poured the last of the liquid from the bottle into another bottle and took these two with me into my room, hiding them in my sock drawer for now. I called the police and waited their arrival. I explained best I could my understanding of the situation. He had returned from a business trip to Russia having had great success and he was in excellent spirits. After showering us with gifts I went to bed. I was awakened by the sound of gunfire and I discovered this scene.

The investigation focused on the two empty glasses and determined the contents of both contained an unknown substance, but the chemistry suggested hallucinates, stimulants and other unidentified organic compounds with unknown properties. The house was eventually searched for more of the liquid, but I had since moved both the incense and my bottle of the liquid out of the house to my grandmother's basement, placing them surreptitiously behind the washing machine amidst a nest of spider webs, dead insects and lost socks.

I awaited the police report to work its way out. They looked into the places my father had visited on his last trip to Russia and I asked for a copy of that list which was eventually given to me. They requested their counterparts in Russia investigate where Benjamin might have come across the substance found in the glasses, but hope of discovering the truth was very dim for them. Too many questions were left unanswered. Too many assumptions had to be made to even begin a pursuit of truth.

I, however, had less doubt. I had Dafna and her words to me. I had complete confidence in my ability to discover the truth. The day of the funerals came and the cadre of family, friends and business associates filed through. This was followed by reading of his will, which bequeathed me the sole heir in the death of both my parents. I worked with our family lawyer to interview firms that would best be qualified to run my father's diverse companies. I left his investments in the hands of the existing portfolio manager. People kept asking how I was holding up. I had no answer for this other than that I was.

I reviewed the list of locations my father was known to visit on his last business trip and the times he was at each, trying to get an idea of where to start. I began to search maps for small spring-fed lakes in the midst of forests near these locations and one answer came up – Tikhvin. Benjamin had purchased a factory in that town during his stay there. I felt it was my best shot at finding an answer, or proving myself capable of perhaps the same madness my father displayed unexpectedly in the final hours of his life. A reckless disregard for safety and pursuit of enlightenment at all costs.

I arrived in Tikhvin and met with a lovely young woman named Alina who would be acting as my translator. She had spent time in American and had a reasonable grasp on English. She had grown up and lived most of her life in Tikhvin. Her hair was shoulder length and had a reddish tint to it that went well with her delicate face, full lips and long eyelashes.

"Hello sir it is such a pleasure to meet you. My name is Alina and I would be happy to show you about my city Tikhvin."

"Alina I am Aaron Blackstone. I am very pleased to meet you." I shook her hand cordially. "I am looking to visit locations my father might have been to while in your city recently. I have a list here of places I know he went to, but this list is likely incompletely."

"I'm sorry, you are looking to find your father in Tikhvin?" She asked struggled to understand me.

"No, I just want to see the same places my father saw when he visited Tikhvin."

"Oh, I see." She laughed at this with a pleasant full faced laugh that made me very comfortable with her. "Would you like to first take the baggage to your lodging before we begin our tour?"

"That sounds wonderful."

We dropped off the bags at a small staid hotel room with an elevator that left me with the desire to use the stairs next time. I met Alina again in the lobby where she awaited me and we began our tour. We hailed a car, which picked us up. Here any driver can take on the roll of taxi should they choose, but in this case the driver was someone she knew quite well. The driver was a burly man with a two day beard, a bald head and always had a cigarette in his hand. He wore Adidas shoes, pants and shirt. She asked if he had time to take us on a tour around the city and after what sounded like a heated argument that went on for some time, during which I held the handle of the door expecting to be issued out at any moment, she turned to me, "Its agreed, it will be Pavel's pleasure to take you about the city today." Pavel turned to me with a big smile filled with three gold teeth and reached out his hand for a firm shake. I settled back in the Lada and we began our tour. Alina explained the history of Tikhvin including its early settlement, its roll is World War II, and its importance due to the Monastery of the Assumption, the primary landmark of the town. We went to see my father's factory and with Alina's help I interviewed the senior staff to learn what my father had done and whom he'd met while he was there. Everyone was excited to meet me and I was greeted with great enthusiasm. What I learned of my father's stay however was limited to business. They did mention he went many times off on his own through the city, though they had offered to have someone accompany him he wished to explore by himself. I recognized the reckless arrogance of my father in these descriptions. He'd often needed time to be off on his own, making his own discoveries both of the world and himself. My mother and I had grown used to this habit long ago and in many ways I had inherited the same trait.

Alina requested that we have dinner with her parents to which I agreed, for best I could tell there were no restaurants in town, only kiosks with groceries and old women on street corners selling their produce and wild mushrooms they had picked. Alina collected goods from both these places and I helped carry them back to the apartment building that her parent's lived in. All these Soviet buildings had the same brooding menace. Strong and effective, but with no external emotion, dark foreboding stairways and, as I mentioned earlier, tiny archaic elevators you expected were operating from below by men turning wheels in the cellars. Inside one of these apartments things brightened up greatly. There was light, music, a television always playing some classic old Soviet film or today's news. A cat named Glosha ran itself between my legs as I tried not to step on it, removing my shoes at the door as required by custom.

"Aaron, this is my mother Galina and my father Sergei. And I see you have met Glosha as well." She then made a joke pointing to the cat and everyone laughed. She continued in Russia introducing me and I held out my hand in greeting. Following introductions, Sergei and I went into the living room and he pointed out his television with great pride. He had almost no English, but Alina would shout from the kitchen to let me know what he was asking from time to time. After showing me his pistol and his uniform from the army he asked if I enjoyed football to which I replied yes and Alina shouted back to her father to go ahead and turn the televisor on to the game. As we watched, he smoked and explained to me things about the team playing, none of which was translated to me so I simply smiled and nodded my head. Glosha came and sat on my leg.. I discovered through trial and error not to pet her as she would bite painfully hard when I did so.

The meal was ready and we went into the cramped kitchen to sit around a very small table as the two women served us the food. Everything was delicious and fresh. The wild mushrooms added a flavor I have craved ever since. After the meal a tort was brought out and we enjoyed dessert with tea. They asked me many questions about why I was in Tikhvin and how proud they were to have the factory in their city. Galina worked in the factory and was thankful for the job. They asked about differences with America, such as did the roads have such bad potholes, to which I answered fortunately no they did not. That appeared to be a sore spot for them as it made driving a slow and frustrating affair around the decaying Tikhvin roadways.

The meal wound down and I thanked them for their hospitality. Alina offered to walk me back to my room, but I insisted I could do it on my own. Sergei felt this was unwise and called a friend to bring by a car to take me there. I acquiesced seeing no way around it and bid them all goodnight.

The following day we toured the local churches, the birthplace of Nikolai Rimsky-Korsakov and finally made our way to the great Assumption Monastery that dominated the culture and history of the town. It was magnificent and decaying, the mixture giving it even more of a dominant feel on the landscape. We passed long-bearded monks and the walkways were surrounded by flowers. In the center was the Assumption church and a copy of the Mother of God icon stood there. Various copies were seen all over and small ones could be purchased. We paid for some candles and lit them within the church as a service was underway.

The actual Mother of God icon was in Chicago having been smuggled out during World War II to elude the German invasion. There was hope it would one day return, but its present keepers awaited stability before they would return the masterpiece.

As the night was setting in I turned down another offer to eat with her parents saying I would rather spend the evening alone contemplating what I had learned. I did, however wonder if there was a small spring-fed lake nearby in a forest that was crystal clear. Her eyes lit up as I mentioned this. "I love this lake it is called Saint Lake and it is so very beautiful. If you would like, I can take you there tomorrow. It is not far from town."

"I would appreciate that very much." And with that my quest for my father's journeys was combined with my curiosity to find any foundation to the strange dream I had during the last hours of his life.

Pavel drove us out of town towards the lake and dropped us off in the midst of nowhere. We began a major hike through the woods during which Alina pointed out interesting landmarks, such as round indentations that could be seen at times where German bombs from World War II had struck the area. As we got into the forest the ground became covered in thick moss and I recalled this sensation from my dream. In the moss, cranberries grew and Alina pointed out as a common pastime of many Russian's to go to the forest to pick cranberries and wild mushrooms. She began to point out the various mushrooms we found on the way and had brought a small knife for each of us and bags for collecting them. She taught me the proper way to slice the mushroom so that it could grow once more from its roots. She also pointed out ways to avoid the deadly mushrooms, which sometimes looked very similar to a safe one.

At long last we came upon the lake. Secluded, breathtaking, pristine and just as I remembered it from my dreams, with the one exception that it was thankfully barren of corpses. Alina removed her shoes and splashed her feet in the coolness of it. "For me this is the most peaceful place in the world." I hesitated to issue her my next question following that statement and thought about how best to rephrase it.

"Has it always been safe out here? I mean, has there ever been any trouble in these woods or near this lake?"

"Oh it is very safe here." She smiled. "The only stories are old ghost stories that make some people stay away from this place at night."

"Can you tell me of these ghost stories?"

"I don't know them very well. I think they are silly. They are about people killing virgins and children here for the devil. These stories are very old."

"Does anyone know more about these ghost stories we could talk to?"

"Actually Pavel does." She laughed heartily at this. "He only agreed to take us out here if we promised to be ready for him to pick us up before it got dark."

We enjoyed the lake some more and I marveled how it matched my dream, the entire area. Making our way back we saw Pavel asleep in his car with popular Russian music playing on his radio. On the trip back Alina questioned him about the old legends of the ghosts. His spirit brightened up and this and he began to tell the tale.

Apparently during the time of Peter the Great, there was a rich man in town named Vasily. He had much farmland and was considered a very important man in the region. Over a series of several nights he suffered losses in his livestock. Some people traveling through town offered to help protect his cattle and goats from further fatalities and he agreed to their offer. Indeed the purge halted and he rewarded them by allowing them to stay and continue to work for him on his farm in various means. A short time later, his only son Alexei grew ill and despite all efforts and expense the boy died. Vasily grew despondent at the loss of his child and turned to drinking. His wife could be of no comfort to him though she insisted they could try for another child. With time she also grew ill and passed. Vasily became more dark in his mood and his temper would flash in public if anyone approached him with a question or to console him for his losses. The workers on his farm began to see strange things happening at night and queer sounds. Soon many of these chose better to leave town and look for new jobs than stay at a place they felt was cursed by the devil himself. So the farmland became untended. The animals roamed free, gaunt and sickly, dying and left to rot where they fell. Complaints were issued, but his influence prevented any action. Over time it no longer resembled a farmland and no one dared to go near it. No one saw Vasily and the only people that were known to associated with him were the strangers that had initially come to help with his lost cattle. This small group and expanded over time without anyone being aware of when. They grew to at least 40 people living up on the farm. How they survived, no one was certain. Certain nights, swarms of bats filled the air, something no one had remembered ever seeing and have never seen since either. Animals began disappearing around town and soon after children and young women went missing first from neighboring rural areas and further villages and finally from within Tikhvin itself. Whether justified or not, people began to suspect satanic rituals happening on Vasily's old farm. They ordered the authorities to do something about it and finally this was done. The lost children and girls were found all murdered on the farm, their bodies eaten by these satanic worshippers that had come to Vasily's farm. Vasily himself had long been dead, having already been one of their victims earlier.

"So what does this have to do with the lake and the forest?"

"All this used to be Vasily's farmland. It was replanted as forest to purge the area of the evil that happened here."

37

"Tell me, is there a place where the victims of this massacre were buried?"

Pavel thought about this and suggested I speak to the monks at the monastery. He knew the monks of the time were involved in cleansing the area of the devil.

"Thank you Pavel, that was a very interesting tale."

Alina translated for Pavel, "You are very welcome. No one cares about this history anymore but you Americans."

I started at this and asked for clarification, "Who else has asked you about these stories?"

Alina translated, "The gentleman who bought the factory in town was very interested. Pavel discussed it with him at great length over many beers."

Tantalized, I pushed further. "Is there anything in particular this man asked that I haven't asked? Is there any further information he was interested in?"

"He asked Pavel if there was anyone who might know about the artifacts of this cult that might have survived. Pavel told him to check with Father Misha at the monastery."

"I also would like to meet this Father Misha. Can that be arranged?"

"Anything can be arranged, this is Russia!"

On the following morning we went to the Assumption Monastery to locate Father Misha. The Russian police were there before us and I suspected they were on the same trail to discover what happened to my father. We found ourselves pushed away because of an investigation they would not explain to us. I tried to have Alina clarify that this might be about my father and I was here to help the search. The officer told us to fuck off and we had no recourse but to leave for the day. We tried again the following day when the police had left, but were turned away at the gate. Father Misha was not seeing guests and there was no one else to discuss anything concerning old ghost stories with us.

I brooded in my room, feeling despondent and at an impasse, trying to decide what was my best way to proceed. A knock came to the door and it was the police. Word of my visits to the monastery had resulted in my visa being revoked. I was being escorted back to Saint Petersburg and sent off on the next flight they could board me on. I hoped that Pavel and Alina would not suffer from their efforts to aid me. I was given no chance to bid them farewell as they pushed me into a car and sped me off to the airport.

Back at my home I stewed at having made such progress but not resolved anything. I made notes and connections and researched what I could find that might have any bearing on the situation, but nothing got me any closer to an answer. I wished I had least found more definitive proof of Dafna or why my father was investigating the same things I had stumbled upon from a dream.

This last thought got me thinking. I took out the box of incense and the bottle of liquid, both of which I had brought backed to my parent's house after the investigation wound down. In inhaled again on the incense, as I had done the first night my father showed it to me and then I breathed in the dark liquid. As I was setting it down, without a thought I dipped it on my finger and then sucked it off. It was bitter, rich, with a burnt taste to it. I hoped my dreams might carry me where Dafna was. I would have laughed at myself were I not so serious in my quest.

The night passed and I lay unable to sleep for some time, my mind too busy with thoughts and connections that led to nothing. Eventually, with a branch tapping out a metronome beat on a distant window of the silent house, I dozed off into a colorful and dark world. I saw the lake again. This time there was no forest, only overgrown fields. A road went near it and continued away towards some distant structures I could only guess were the farm houses of Vasily. Beside the lake there was a series of torches burning and in the midst of the torches were people dressed in white gowns. At least some where in white gowns, other were nude and covered in blood. Some were in the midst of passionate sex, but the real draw to my attention was the man positioned upon a stone that glowed with an inner light with a long blade issuing from his chest. Beside him was another glowing stone covered in blood and from which a body was being rolled off to join a terrifying collection of corpses already amassed there. Then I noticed someone looking directly at me. It was Dafna and she was a dressed in white. They tore this from her as she kept her eyes locked on me, tears began to run down her face. They pushed her back to stand against the edge of the stone and they plunged the strange blade into her chest. She gasped and fell to her knees, blood running from the edges of her mouth and her eyes momentarily left their lock from me. She looked up at me once more and whispered, "Follow the stones. Wherever they go, madness reigns." They pressed her body against the stone and forced the blade deeper inside of her. Her body fought and her hands and feet clenched, she sighed out as life gave way from her.

The next morning I held the strange blade in my hands that my father had brought back with him on his last trip. It was as I had seen it in the dream. A long silver handle ending in five blades set in a circular patter. In the dream these were used to pierce the heart of the victim upon the stones. I pressed it carefully against my own chest to see how it aligned around the human heart. I pulled it from me quickly and tossed it away, wave of fear gripping me.

I poured considerable funds into hiring people to research the time of Peter the Great, the region of Tikhvin, the Assumption Monastery and anything concerning a wealthy landowner named Vasily or a girl named Dafna. The information began to stream in and I hired others to sort and categorize it for me. Laura was my main staff person and would summarize the findings for me. I told them I was working on a book and this was research. I made donations anonymously to the monastery in Tikhvin through a nonprofit I set up to save Orthodox holy places. I contacted Alina and put her in charge of this nonprofit and to set forward work restoring the monastery. We provided the money in small sums directly hiring labor to avoid corruption. I worried Alina was taking a risk so I asked her to be unconnected as possible with the money and not directly contact the monastery as herself, but send others on her behalf.

These efforts took time and money, and were weak on results for some time. We found evidence of the land near the lake having been farmed by someone, but the information on this had been lost as the estate and land was taken back in 1717. It was six months later with the help of Alina researching in Saint Petersburg that we had our breakthrough. She discovered in archives a shipping manifest that included cargo from Tikhvin and the estate of Vasily Pasternack. The Apostle Peter had set sail from Saint Petersburg stopping port in Copenhagen and then not stopping again until it sank just off the coast of Cameroon. I kissed her across the phone for this information and she laughed happily for such good news after so much effort. "But since the ship sank is it not a dead end?"

"Maybe, maybe not. But I'm going there to find out. Thank you my dear and don't think you've heard the last of me! I will be in touch again when I can."

"Goodbye Aaron and please be safe on your journey. I want to hear your voice again soon."

"I promise you will. Be well Alina."

I hung up phone and called Laura. "Its Aaron. We have a new lead. I'm sending you information on a ship that sank off the coast of Cameroon in 1717. We need to find out all we can about this ship, what it was holding, why it sank and if any of the crew and cargo made it to shore."

We scoured research centers and libraries for information on the ship and its sinking along with the events of Cameroon at that time and after. There was nothing, nothing at all. Nothing until we looked over a 100 years later when a devilish sex cult was described as sacrificing animals, children and people in bloody drug induced ceremonies. This cult was attacked and massacred in 1821 according to records. Since then nothing similar was spoken of.

With this fresh information we adjusted our research to fan out anywhere we could find information on cults, satanic rituals, sacrifices of animals and people, and any mention of this on stones or with incense and drug use. We centered the search around West Africa and any ports that ships leaving from 1821 or on might have headed. This was easily the longest part of our search. It was another year and a half before Laura sat before me the list of potentials that had not been ruled out by additional research into the validity of their claims.

"This third one, the one in America, it stands up to scrutiny?"

"That one actually had the most third party validation in the form of eye witness reports. But that is not what makes it interesting. What's fascinating is that these events take place on the Stafford estate and the son of the estate owner was in the Gold Coast just prior to returning home."

"Laura, this is amazing. We've got to get down to Georgia immediately."

Milledgeville was where everything became clear. I haven't had time to write all that I have learned because it has been happening so fast. I promise to take time when it presents itself to properly detail this critical portion of the journey. For now there is only time to push forward with what has been learned and try to prevent something unspeakable, unthinkable that I believe is on the verge of happening.

This morning was Easter service at the First Baptist Church of Woodstock Georgia. I had made myself a prominent member six months earlier. Giving lavishly, greeting congregants, involving myself in projects and generally getting the appropriate people familiar with my face and my reliability. As was my occasional custom, I stopped in by the infants to check on Lydia and see if she needed any assistance with a particular colicky baby.

"They are so well behaved today I don't know what to do with myself."

"Lovely to hear that." I enacted my plan to alter that scenario, handing some toy blocks to several babies and pulling a few extra from my sleeve to hand to two in particular.

"How has your brother been Lydia, any improvement in the last week?"

She turned to me with sagging shoulders, "It's so hard to watch this strong man fade away before my eyes. I know its God's will, but I pray every day his condition will turn."

"I know how hard that can be Lydia. I went through it with the long painful loss of my father, rest his soul." By this point the first child was in tears and red faced. The second child wore a stunned uncertain look on his face as he processed the unfamiliar taste that I had coated the blocks with. Soon he was crying as well.

"Uh oh, here we go." Lydia rushed to the children, picking up the girl first.

"Here let me help you with this one." I offered, picking up the boy and bouncing him gently in my arms. "There there child. No worries. Everything is alright. Shhhhhh shhhhhh." But the bawling from either was not going to stop for the sting was still in their mouths.

"Oh poor baby! What is wrong with you sweetie?" Lydia danced about with the girl.

"Lydia, I am going to walk him down the hall and see if I can entertain him with the water fountain. That often works I've found."

"Okay Marshall, thank you so much for being such a dear." I left the room and gave the child a pacifier that would quickly ease the inflammation within his mouth. He calmed down in a short time and watched the water fountain with great fascination. Once he was appropriately quiet I handed him another toy from my pocket that I knew would intrigue him for at least a few minutes as I slipped out the side door of the building and pulled the keys to the Jetta I had parked there. Placing the infant in the carseat in the back, I entered the car and exited the parking lot taking a back road and a circuitous route back to the Kroger lot where I had left my Mercedes. I knew time would be short, but the plans were already all in place. I moved the child from the Jetta to the carseat in the back of the Mercedes and wiped my prints off the Jetta. Heading back on the road I drove the rest of the way to Hartsfield Airport, boarding a direct flight on Delta to Saint Petersburg Russia for myself, Douglas Arkwright, and my infant son Jonathan, both of which I had the appropriate papers and Visas at hand.

It is on this flight that I am writing this now. I defend my actions with the fullest of my might. There was no other way to prevent this child's gruesome death at the hands of diabolical forces that care for nothing but themselves.

Alina met me at Pulkovo Airport in Saint Petersburg. I handed the child to her wide amazed eyes.

"Oooh, he's so beautiful. I cannot believe it. Hello Jacob, I'm Alina nice to meet you my sweetheart." The baby smiled back at her, drooling with big bright eyes.

Pavel had the car ready for us and we all entered the Lada to head back to Tikvin.

"Privyet Aaron!"

"Privyet Pavel, long time no see my friend."

"Aaron, please what is your plan with the child? Why did you bring him to Russia?" Alina asked from the back where she sat beside Jacob's child seat.

"I'm hoping we can get some help from the monks at the Assumption Monastery. They dealt with Vasily and I am hoping if we can convince them this is happening yet again, we can get them to reveal what they did to stop it before. Someone has to have this information, I just know it."

Alina contacted the monastery for us and arrange a meeting with Father Avraamy. Father Misha, we discovered, had died unexpectedly soon after the police had visited the monastery in the early days of our research. Father Avraamy was delighted to finally get to meet the benefactor that had been supporting renovations for the past few years. We schedule a meeting for two days after my arrival and we headed up to Assumption Monastery with Jacob at hand. Alina doted happily over the baby and he took to her immediately.

Father Avraamy met us in his office and greeted us with warmth and great enthusiasm. He wore a full black habit with an Orthodox cross hanging across his chest. His grey beard went down past his shoulders. His Kalymafki was stiff and dramatic on his head. He went on at great length about the improvements they had been able to perform owing to my generous support, including much needed reconstruction, repainting of the monastery walls and desperately needed repairs for ceilings that had been leaking.

I begged him not to mention it as it was for such a worthy cause in the name of God. I then set down the silver dagger upon his desk, holding it there for a moment while maintaining his gaze and then pushing it forward to sit right in front of him at his desk. "You know what this is. I know it was kept safe here and somehow found its way out along with these items." I placed the box of incense and the bottle of tonic on the table as well, opening each for him to view. "These items were purchased near here several years ago by my father and they led to the death of both my parents."

Recovering from his initial shock at seeing the blade, Father Avraamy stood up from the table and boisterously defended his ignorance of such things, going on how if I came here to accuse them of some diabolical efforts that ended in the death of his parents he would gladly take down all the paint and repairs I had paid for and give them back to me, for he had no spot on his soul for such accusations.

"We know about Vasily and the roll this monastery had in his destruction. There is a second Vasily in the making and this child represents our only hope in stopping it."

These words stopped the Father cold in his temper and he paused to look at the child for a moment, finally walking over and requested Alina let him hold him.

"Why do you insist this child will stop a new Vasily?"

"Because 150 years ago his ancestor was set to be sacrificed but this was interrupted. I believe this child has been chosen as a surrogate for his ancestor to complete the sacrifice and without him, it cannot be done."

Father Avraamy returned the child and began to pace wildly about the room, having been quite agitated by what he'd expected to be a simple meeting to kiss ass of a major benefactor. "I don't know what you come here and expect from me."

"I expect answers and information. What we've done, we've done blind and on our own. We know there are answers here, I can feel it in my bones. I don't want to have lost my parent's for nothing. I want to prevent harm from coming to this child."

"And how to do propose to do that?"

"By keeping him here. They can't touch him here."

"And how can you be so sure!?" Avraamy thundered, his face red and shuddering. "You know nothing of what you are doing! You bring this child here

43

endangering us all with your arrogant beliefs! There is no out from what has been set! The only way you can save this child from what you fear for it –" He paused in his rage to lean himself against his desk and recover his breath. In a quieter voice he continued as he sat himself back down in his chair. "The only way to save him, is to take his life with your own hands. There is no other answer. As long as he lives, he is marked for this purpose and the walls of this holy sanctuary are no barrier to them at all, regardless of what you have been led to believe."

I was taken aback by his outburst. I had not expected anything of the sort. I turned to Alina who looked at me with equal concern. Jacob slept calmly against her arm and she held him closely to herself. I found myself realizing a deep attraction to her, something that might have been there before had I but noticed it. "Father Avraamy, I beg you please let us keep the child here at least for now so we can discuss with you the best recourse to move forward."

Father Avraamy, physically and emotionally exhausted, waved his hand in agreement and also to issue us away from him so he could have time to think on his own. We left the old man and I looked back once more as we exited the room to see his eyes deep in thought. The sensation this gave me was of great hope for all of my future and that of Jacob depended on the wisdom and knowledge of this man.

A room was arranged for Jacob and myself, and Alina helped settle us in. She seemed torn about leaving and I wanted her to stay myself, but I did not speak of this feeling. She bid us goodnight and headed back to her apartment in town.

I settled in after feeding Jacob and getting him bedded for the night, and wrote down the experiences of the day in this journal. At 2 in the morning a knock came upon the door and awoke me. It was Father Avraamy carrying a lantern and a stern look on his face. He beckoned me to follow, our communication limited without Alina to translate for us. I was nervous about leaving Jacob by himself and I ushered Avraamy's attention to the child. He motioned for me to bring the boy. I carefully picked Jacob up so not to wake him, laying him against my shoulder, and followed Avraamy into the night. We went out into the courtyard and into the Assumption Church at its center. Other monks were present there and he directed me to hand Jacob off to one of them which I reluctantly did. He started to wake up and fuss, but the monk began to sing and rock him back to rest upon his shoulder. Candlelight and the lantern were the only illumination at this hour and the haunting echoes as we walked in the great open spaces were striking within the deep shadows around us, no sounds to be heard but our footsteps. We went to a side door into an area used for storage and cleaning supplies and then to another door beyond this room. This door had a heavy lock upon it and Father Avraamy drew out the key to open it. Once this was done, he led me within by his small lantern's glow. Inside was a very small room with a tight metal spiral staircase leading downwards. He began to descend this and I followed him. It was colder down here and very damp. There was a thin corridor leading ahead of us and we began to make our way down this. The floor grew slick and the walls were shiny. Touching the brick I discovered it was slime. There was light flickering ahead of us that grew brighter as we continued our approach. I could see torches set apart from each other in a semicircle as we finally entered a room at the end of the corridor. My breath left me at what I saw in the midst of the torches. Heavy chains hung from either wall and held aloft the arms of a man — or what was left of a man. His skin was dark and grey with slime covered him as well. His head was hairless and hung limply forward. He had no clothes on. From below his waist, his body was missing. In his chest five daggers had been thrust in a circle around his heart.

Father Avraamy brought his lantern close to the body and looking at me simply said, "Vasily".

As I stared at the corpse in horror, it raised its head to look at him. Vasily's jaw had been ripped from his face and what was left of his tongue fell freely across his neck. He eyes had been gouged out and a crucifix was thrust into the right one as well as the right ear. Avraamy began to shout in dismay and screamed at me waving his hand for me to leave. As terrified as I was of this abomination I was uncertain I wanted to find my way in the dark down that corridor and up those stairs. Avraamy searched the floor with his lantern and found a crucifix and then a second one. He approached the demon who struggled from him as he came near. Avraamy ushered me over and handed me the lantern so he could grab the wretch by its head and thrust a crucifix into its left socket and the other within the canal of its left ear. This done he grabbed the lantern from me and rushed back down the corridor and up the staircase. He was shouting to the monks as we were only half way up and several came running to his call. There followed a heated discussion with monk's issuing from the scene with instructions as the drama unfolded. Finally Avraamy turned to me and simply shouted, "Alina!" grabbing me by the hand and pulling me to a phone. I rang her up at not 3 in the morning and she finally answered.

"Alina, its Aaron. I'm sorry to bother you but something is happening –" Avraamy wrenched the phone from my hand and began speaking feverishly to her. Once he was finished he slammed down the phone and left the church in a flurry. Jacob was in the church still being held by a priest. I waited in the church the next few hours as the sun prepared to rise. Alina spent much of this time with me and Jacob, but was called back by Father Avraamy periodically. Finally Alina entered again with Father Avraamy. Her face was pained with worry.

"Aaron, there is much trouble, we are going to have to leave. Something terrible has happened I am not sure what it is, but Father says it is something that has never happened before." I was certain this was in references to the crucifixes that were either dislodged or removed from Vasily in the dungeon below. "Father asks me to give you this, it is to guard your protection." She handed me a silver chain with a circular silver cage at the end. It was heavy, filled with something inside the cage and the cage felt cool and wet. "It is dipped in holy water."

Another monk came into the church with news and Father Avraamy turned to the other priests and to Alina for further discussion before he followed after to attend to this new business. Alina turned to me again, "The police are here. They are looking for Jacob."

Everything was breaking down so fast. How could they possibly have worked through all the ruse and deception I had set up in coming here to find us? The panic showed on my face and she grabbed me by my arms to face her.

"Aaron, you must leave with Jacob now! There is a tunnel passage that goes to the Tikhvinka river and there is a small boat there you can use to get to the other side. I will ask Pavel to wait for you there and he will take you both somewhere far that Father says will be safe, the only safe place he trusts for you now." She kissed me on the cheek tenderly. "Hurry Aaron, there is no time."

I took Jacob and was led to the tunnel. Jacob fussed in the tunnel at being awakened again and I feared we would be heard from above. The tunnel went on for some time before we saw the first lights of dawn sparkling on the Tikhvinka. Outside the tunnel the first thing I noticed was the bats. Dozens of bats circling the skies. Once I placed him inside the boat Jacob calmed down and we were able to quietly row across the river to the far shore. The bats circled above us and began to land upon the boat. I swung at them with my paddle, but they moved easily to avoid my strikes. I kept padding and more bats boarded our vessel, approaching the child and looking at him. I paddled faster, seeing Pavel's rusty brown Lada pulling up just ahead of where I was destined. He started to usher at me as I drew near and more of the winged rats crowded the boat. He was waving an arm in the air and I didn't understand his meaning. Finally he removed his belt and swung it about his head and I got the idea of what he was meaning. I stopped my paddling and drew out the chain Alina had given me and began to swing it around my head. It whistled and spread water out of it. The cloud immediately flew from the boat. I placed it back down and I paddled harder to reach the shore. The bats began to dive at me scratching and clawing at my back and reaching for my face. The boat hit the shore and Pavel jumped into the water to grab up Jacob. I began madly swinging the chain about me again and the fiends backed away from us. We piled into the Lada and started feverishly down the road.

I fell asleep during the drive and woke to find we were still traveling. Eventually we came to another monastery, this one Pskov Caves Monastery which was breathtaking in its grandeur. Father Alexander met us on arrival and spoke with Pavel. We were ushered into the monastery and given a room to rest in. We ate and I collapsed into another deep sleep for an unknown time.

We've spent the last five weeks here now and I haven't heard from Alina or Pavel or Father Avraamy. There is no one here who speaks English to me and we are ushered away as the public comes through the tour the monastery. It has become a lonely life, but we appear to be safe. I look to the sky for bats every day and breath a relief when there is nothing out of the ordinary.

I take time now to recount some of what we learned in Milledgeville. The blood cult that we had heard word of in Cameroon, was indeed broken up in an Islamic Jihad in 1821, but some of the members were sold off as slaves and a few ended up in Milledgeville on the Stafford plantation. They appeared to have initiated the son of Obediah Stafford into their cult and he sailed to the Gold Coast and recovered artifacts from Cameroon belonging to the cult. These artifacts were then used within a ceremony that wasn't allowed to end due to intervention of Union troops on the plantation. The two survivors were Jacob Anderson and Idaliah Madison. It took us considerable time to get these names as the archives in Milledgeville had lost almost all records of the two. Both these survivors spent time in the Central State Hospital due to their inability to recall their own names or recognize faces of relatives and close friends. It took years of therapy to return them to a stable enough condition to be released back into society. They were not the only ones to have reports at Central State and we learned more about what might have happened that night on the plantation. Tales of mass killing of the insane and slaves as well as Obediah Stafford himself along with his son Aquilla. Swarms of crows, tales of lions and jackals, not dissimilar to the stories we heard in Cameroon and in Tikhvin. We eventually discovered that Jacob had two children later in life and Idaliah three. We followed these trees and interviewed the descendants, none of whom where aware of the events or the names of their distant ancestors. And then we found baby Jacob Skyler, descendent of Jacob Anderson. I hired a detective named Mackerlin to watch the Skyler house for us and follow wherever the child went, taking photos and especially watching out for any crows in the trees. The first four reports showed normal family behavior yet an ever presence of at least two crows that appeared to follow wherever he went. When Mackerlin called me one night in a panic claiming crows were now following him as well, I told him to leave the case and paid him handsomely to take a far off vacation. I had enough to coerce my easily convincible mind that this child was important and went about the task of securing his future survival.

Today is to be my final journal entry. I can feel the end coming upon me already. I am seated out in the lush field of the monastery, Jacob playing in the grass beside me. Across from us, on the other side of the monastery walls, sitting on the branch of a tree was what I thought to be a squirrel staring at me. But it sat motionless for such a time I noticed its tail was far too long for a squirrel. Indeed I could now make out it was a monkey. As I leaned up just now to take a closer look, I found my legs had gone numb and I knew that was why he was watching me. This was Aquilla's monkey familiar Mephisto, renown for his poisonings. And he had gotten to me. Even within the walls of this most sacred place he had found a way to poison me. I thought about how he might have done it. Was it the soup? Was it the wine I had earlier with the meal? No. I knew as the pain grabbed my insides and wrenches them in a circle. It was the apple.

My sweet sweet Aaron. How I miss you my love. My world has collapsed since they killed you. I have not the strength to get out of bed each morning. I feel betrayed by God, by the world. How could they take you, you who were so very good? You who gave all of yourself for others. I felt such respect for you the minute I saw you. I knew this was a man like none other I had ever met. I was afraid to share such feelings for you, you being so handsome and so well off and I such a simple girl from such a simple town. When I read your journal and saw what you wrote about me, my eyes burst in tears. I screamed at the pages how much I loved you. I tore at my clothes and pounded my hands against the wall to know I could never say these words to you. I love you Aaron. I love you with all my heart. No one can ever replace the hole you leave in me. I miss you so terribly my love.

They took Jacob away. He has been returned to his parents. I don't know how to continue the fight for you. I do not have your resources or your strength. Without you I am certain the child is lost and this breaks my heart once again. It feels like losing you all over again to know that I cannot protect the child you sacrificed your life for.

I've consoled myself by learning all I could about Vasily and the girl you saw in your dreams, Dafna. You would be pleased to learn I found her. She is buried in Tikhvin beside her mother and father. I keep her grave clean and place flowers there as I know you would have done had you been given the chance to see that she was real. I feel so close to her, the woman who died so very long ago such a horrible death. I feel close because she spoke to you. She brought you to me. Without her you may never have come to Tikhvin and I never would have had the chance to meet you. She is my greatest comfort in these hard days. I feel most calm when I am pulling weeds and planting fresh flowers for her. I tell her about you and how good a person you were. How hard you tried to follow her words, how much we both tried to honor her memory and prevent others from feeling the pain that she felt in her life. I pray somewhere the two of you have now met and watch over me now. Perhaps you will speak to me in my dreams and teach me how I can continue the work you both held with such passion. Someday I hope to meet you both in a better place where such pain as I feel today is a distance memory.

Yours in truest love, Alina.

Part III
Vasily

Vasily lay in his bed, not having moved for hours. At this point he was just awaiting the word, which came as the doctor entered the bedroom. The dour look on the man's face answering the inevitable. Ludmilla was no more. His beautiful wife, the moon and the sun of his world had gone. The body of his boy Vanya might still be warm, having passed less than a day ago and his dearest mother three days prior to that. He had no will to go on. There was no purpose to drive his limbs, to push his heart to beat. For what do his lungs breath in air when all that he cared for in this world had grown cold. Why not take him as well? Why spare him to watch helplessly as everything good was consumed by the grave and he was left to stand helplessly by, thrashing his chest and begging to be taken in their place.

He could not hear what the doctor was saying to him as he stood over his bed. He simply waited for him to leave, leave him to his eternal misery. He thought of the swollen bulge of endless painful time he must suffer through ahead of him. Alone with is regret, his loss, his agony. The doctor continued to speak and he knew the whoreson was staggering on with some pompous advice or consolation. Enraged, Vasily grabbed the lamp from the beside table and cast it full force against the man's face. The glass shattered and blood sprayed from the torn cheek as the old quack stumbled backwards. Vasily standing upon his bed and shouting obscenities and hate, his fists clenched in balls and drool rolling down his chin as he fought back his tears of pain.

He stood there upon his bed bent upright by unrestrained rage and pain for time untold, his heart pounding wildly and his muscles flexed to fight – fight against anything that would just let him fight back! He became aware that Oksana, one of the house servants, stood before him quietly. He shouted at her to leave, pouring his abuse on her with abundance, wishing she would follow the rest of them to the grave, why should she be exempt, what does she know of loss? "If you don't leave my room right now I will slit your throat myself with this broken lamp at your feet and drink your blood as you die here! Leave me!!!"

She did not leave but dared to come closer to him. He fumed further at her, his face red and his legs shaking with exhaustion. She ventured to grab him and he collapsed in her hold. She pulled him down to the bed as he heaved for breath and moaned with agony. She dipped a cloth in water from the bowl beside his bed and wiped the sweat from his face. He was too tired to fight her. He let her do as she will. "Vasily. I know how much you hurt my sweet. But all is not lost. Where

Arkady failed I can still save her."

"What rubbish are you speaking, you shit-covered harpy! She's lost to me. They are all lost!"

"No, not lost Vasily. She is merely missing. Even your son is merely missing. I can return them to you if you just allow me to."

"Return? From the grave? Are you the Messiah? Do you have the ear of God?"

"I have more than the ear of God, I have His touch. You have only to trust me my lord."

"Why pain me with false hopes woman!? They are gone, cold and turning to dust as we speak!"

"They are not dust yet. They are not beyond my powers, but they soon will be. You must allow me to act now."

"Act! Go act! I allow it you insufferable bitch! Bring them all back. Go to the cemetery and bring back my father and mother as well. Bring back my uncle Misha while you are at it. Bring back them all, we shall roast a pig and drink around the fire tonight, laughing from the joys of your great action!"

"You mock me, but I beg you to believe me."

He shot up in bed and grabbed her by the neck. "Believe?! Believe in what? My God that has stolen everything from me? Arkady whose medicines did nothing to stop their suffering? Your lies of life beyond death?"

"I have no lies for you. I only offer you the truth."

He stared at her as he held his grip on her throat. She showed no fear to him though he could kill her right then and there. He released and pushed her from him. "Do as you will. I have no faith in your words, but do as you will. Just leave me now or I will beat you with my belt until you walk with a limp! Leave!"

The familiar smell of blini came to Vasily the following morning. He smiled in his sleep imaging his beloved in the kitchen making the special dish that only she could make for him, not the house cooks who were fools. He started upright in his bed, the gorgeous odors still wafting their way to him. He rushed from the room, throwing open his bedroom door and ran frantically for the kitchen. There she stood, in his favorite day dress that hugged her perfect figure and always left him desperate for her in his arms. Her long curly dark hair flowing back behind her. He could practically smell her from across the room she was so remarkably there. "Luda?" His voice could barely say her name, he felt dizzy, confused, hopelessly praying this was all not just a dream.

"Are you hungry my Vasya?" With these words she turned to him and he beheld the face of his beloved, no longer weak and marked with small pox, but as he knew her – young, beautiful and with eyes that discerned his every thought.

He burst out in tears and rushed towards her, pulling her deep into his arms

51

so that she dropped her wooden spoon. He lifted her from the ground and breathed in the scent of her hair. Setting her back down he dappled her with kisses as she laughed from the affection. He put his hands about her face and just stared at her, tears coursing down his cheeks, his hands and lips shaking uncontrollably from fervid emotion. "I lost you."

She took his hand from her face and gently kissed his palm three times. "I came back to you my love."

He stared at her unbelieving, fighting with the reality of her body, her voice, her scent against the knowledge that she had faded, scarred gruesomely, and died the most foul agonizing of deaths just hours before. Yet now she was here, before him, he explored her body, face, hands — all so intimately familiar to him. "How is this possible?"

"Oksana, she grabbed me from the abyss and brought me back to you." She kissed his cheek. The smell of burning blini wafted from the stove and she laughed and ran from him to continue preparing their breakfast. He rushed over and pushed the pan from the flame and grabbed her once again in his arms fiercely.

"How could she do this? It's not possible! You are completely cured, but you had died! I had lost you Ludishka!"

"I don't know what she did. I only saw her come for me and I was able to open my eyes and breath again. I burst out in tears as you are now and wept at her feet kissing them in gratitude."

"Where is Oksana so that I may thank her as well?" He held her tightly against him unable to let go, she felt of everything he desired in the world. He wanted this moment to never end.

"She was too spent from the effort. She collapsed before me. I had her rushed to Arkady to recover."

"Arkady?! That charlatan? He did nothing to save you or Vanya! I should have strangled that louse when I had the chance."

"Oksana needs him now. She's given so much of herself for us to be together again."

"What of Vanya? She promised she could return my son as well."

"She became too weak to complete his reparation and now time is growing short for us if we want him returned to us. We only have one way Vaska and we must do it together."

"Anything! I will give my life for my dear boy!"

She kissed him again. "We must give more than that to have him back my love, but we need to hasten before it is too late."

He stood before Lake Ludmilla on his property. He had named it after her for it was beautiful and she loved it. Behind him a ring of torches burned in the midst of which had been set two large stones. In his hand he held a flagon filled with an unfamiliar pungent beverage, in the other he held a bag of metal cups from the house she had provided him. He awaited her return as he watched the flickering torchlight play across the face of the water. The corpse of his son lay bundled near his feet and covered with a blanket. He could not bring himself to unwrap the body and look at the mottled face of his precious Vanya. He pointed his eyes skyward, gazing into the cloudless star-rich black of the sky. He knew not whether to pray or curse his God, for he was not certain if Ludmilla's return was by His will or against it.

Across the field approached a procession. He felt the play of destiny in their approach. The clock of time was being wound tightly this night. There would be a before and after, the course of this evening would split these blendlessly in two. The weight of it dropped him to his knees. He placed the flagon and the bag on the grass beside him and cast his face into his hands, breathing the smell of them deep into his nostrils, wanting to remember the reek of his flesh.

The line of children approached the lake. They were young boys and girls from the orphanage accompanied by Dafna, their caretaker. Ludmilla ushered them all to seat themselves comfortably about the lake. She brought with her a basket and handed out Pirozhki to everyone. The children ate hungrily of the pies. She ran her hand gently across Vasily's face and asked him to help her hand out the cups to the children. Taking the flagon she began to fill each of their cups with the strong licorice scented drink. Dafna thanked Ludmilla for her kindness and directed the children in singing a song to their hosts for the hospitality. Ludmilla poured a larger cup for herself and handed a similar one to Vasily, lifting it to his mouth and watching until he had downed it completely. She did the same as the children finished their song and drank of their cups as well. The night grew quiet again as the tonic took affect. The children and Dafna grew drowsy and disoriented. Some began to sing a new song about the stars sparking in the ripples of a lake. Ludmilla pressed herself against Vasily and kissed him along his neck to his ear where she whispered of her devotion to him. She took him by the hand into the circle of torches. The scent of their burn filled him with sudden uncontainable desires and he flung her down upon the ground, her head striking harshly against the stone below them. She moaned and reached her hand around his neck to passionate kiss him, biting his tongue until it bled as he held her hands down and began to hump her through their clothes. Frenzied he ripped at her dress and undid his trousers, pressing himself within her and pushing her face to the side to hold her down against the stone as he thrust in and out of her in desperation of desire. He choked her and she clawed at his face as he spread her legs open to accept him deeper. He finally climaxed with a cry and collapsed on top of her panting. She pushed him off of her and went to another bag. He saw blood trailing from the back of her head where she'd struck the stone. She came back dressed in a white dress and held a long odd silver blade with multiple prongs in her hand. She straddled him where he lay across the stone and ran her hands across his face and through his hair. She then lifted the queer blade above her head and sank it into his chest. He gasped in surprise, but not in pain. He felt something he could not describe as she pressed it deeper through his chest. He felt it surrounding his heart and he was no longer able to move.

Ludmilla went over to the children and led one of them, disoriented and crying, to the second stone, where she lay the girl down and thrust a similar blade through her chest. He watched the girl struggle and attempt to call out weakly before going completely limp. Ludmilla withdrew the blade and pulled the girl by her arm from the stone, leaving a trail of blood in wake. This act continued through the night as sixteen orphans were impaled one after the other. At the end she brought Dafna to the stone, tearing her dress from her to reveal her young perfect form and stabbed her through the heart, dropping her to the stone and pressing her weight against the struggling girl until she struggled no longer.

Once this was completed, the stones burned with an internal fire of their own and Oksana returned to Vasily to wrench the blade from his chest. She dropped to her knees before him, exhausted, panting for breath, blood soaking her white dress through. Vasily opened his eyes and turned to her. She prostrated herself before him, "My lord, I am here to do your every bidding. Do with me as you will." Vasily rose from the stone and looked upon her. Grabbing her by her left arm he lifted her into the air and with his free hand tore the dress from her. He struck he harshly across her cheek and flung her to the ground, pulling her to him and began to violently fuck her. She took his punishment with pleasure and layers upon layers of interleaving pain. He thrust himself within her relentlessly, beating her senseless with his fists and bruising her vagina until it bled openly. And yet he plunged on and on within her unconscious form, deep into the night only leaving her hours later to shiver in the chill pre-dawn air, aching and bleeding, but filled with an inextinguishable bliss of accomplishment.

Vasily sat on a charred chair in what had been the Holy of Holies of a small Orthodox church surrounded by a cemetery. His receding hairline and dark piercing eyes soaking in the knowledge of his myriad familiars. The insides of the church were now completely burned out, the once ornate walls scarred deep with black soot from the intense flames. The floor was collapsed, in front of him was great deep hole of rocky rubble that must be carefully crossed if one dared to come near him. From what was left of the ceiling hung hundreds of bats. Amidst the rubble, thousands of dark rats and dozens of wild dogs. Outside the desecrated church, before its charred front door, seven spikes held the heads of monks from the Assumption Monastery that had come the day before to stop the diabolical murder and brutality that had issued from this place for the past few days. The road leading from the church was lined with crosses hung with naked corpses of men and women each with a sign about their necks reading "Join or die".

The bats, rats and dogs continually issued in and out of the debased church scouring the countryside for movement. Most of the residents were either dead or managed to flee into the Assumption Monastery, though many were seduced by the promises of everlasting life and immeasurable pleasures by the growing congregation of followers led by Oksana that worshipped at the feet of Vasily. The stones were set on the far side of the church surrounded in torches and swamped in a continually refreshed pool of blood from endless rituals creating more and more of the terrible demon-beasts that were the eyes, hands and teeth of Vasily. Beside the stones his worshippers endlessly fucked each other and captives they brought here to pleasure themselves with as they murdered them slowly, feeding their corpses to the wild dogs who in turn were used to create yet more monsters.

A group of young men led by a dark-haired 23 year old named Maxim did their best to fight back against the accursed cult and their hellish minions. They helped bring the old and young to the church, braving the showering attacks of bats and the hundreds of rats that scoured the countryside. But it was the cult members and the wild dogs that concerned them most. They were poorly armed, but jealously brave of their city and were willing to sacrifice everything for their loved ones. They bore crosses and carried flagons of holy water to keep the monsters at bay, but these had no impact on those of their own people that had turned to join Vasily.

On their way with two families including five young children to bring to the Monastery they were confronted by Zakhar and five other cult members.

"Where are you going with our dog food?" Zakhar had several of the worst of the wild dogs at his side. He held a machete and his crew were armed with various hand-made or stolen weapons.

Maxim had six in his crew, but protecting the families and the children would be very difficult in this situation. He leaned back to consult with the others. "Ignat, you and Evgeny have to keep the holy water on those mongrels, the rest of you we have to confront these sows and send them back to Vasily in pieces." With his plan set, Maxim gave a great shout and charged Zakhar head on. Zakhar had expected the fear of his hell hounds to petrify Maxim and his crew, but the beasts fell back from the spray of holy water. Maxim shoved the rusted sword of his grandfather through Zakhar and pulled it back out to threaten the others. His comrades charge pushed them back and the remaining cult members fell away.

Zakhar lay gasping on the ground as Maxim stood near him panting from breath, adrenalin flowing from the first time he'd mortally wounded a man. His mind coming back to him, he went back to shouting orders. "C'mon! We must get to the monastery before they regroup."

The walls of the Assumption Monastery kept the beasts at bay and anyone known to have joined the satanic cult were barred from entry, though they pissed, shit and flung obscenities at its gates to the terrified people within. Food was growing scarce as the storage of supplies dwindled. Riders had managed to set out towards Saint Petersburg for help from the king and to Novgorod to the holy fathers there who held knowledge of the last time such a peril had beset Russia.

Maxim led his group and the families to the walls of the Monastery and called up for support. A rope ladder was cast down for them to climb up. This took time, especially for the younger children. As the last of the families and his crew made it up, Maxim turned to see a swirling ball of bats and a streaming flow of rats on their way towards him. "Ignat! Throw me the flagon of holy water!"

"No Maxim, climb the ladder, they can't approach the wall. You can't face them alone."

"Ignat, throw it to me!"

Ignat obeyed and toss the flagon down to Maxim who opened it and prepared for the onslaught approaching him. Marksman on the walls of the Monastery prepared to support him.

"Hello little devils, come to play some more with Maxim? A curse on each of you, you have no right to approach God's sacred home!"

The wall of bats parted to show Vasily standing alone, with rats crawling about his feet.

"Maxim you think God can protect you on either side of that wall? He has no interested in your confidence. You are just a stupid boy who has listened to his mother too much." Vasily walked forward. Ignat cried for Maxim to climb the ladder before it was too late. The marksmen opened fire, but had no impact on Vasily.

"You, who have sold your soul to utter darkness, Vasily. How dare you come near this most holy of God's houses."

"God's houses are my treasures as well Maxim my beautiful boy. You really should come and see His house that I live in now."

"You defile the sacred with your breath!"

"There is no sacred Maxim, not for you, not for any of them hiding behind those walls. There is only me, nothing else."

Maxim's heart told him this was a fight he could not win and climbed the ladder back into the monastery.

"Let's talk again soon young Maxim. I am hoping very soon my good friend."

The first of the riders to make it to their destination was Pyotr, younger brother of Dafna who had joined the monastery at twelve. Now fifteen with a bright head of blonde hair, he reached the great Yuriev Monastery in Novgorod. Father Pimen met him at the door and they discussed the siege of Vasily upon Tikhvin. A meeting was assembled with Abbot Sylvester in attendance.

"This dark spirit has taken over Tikhvin and driven the surviving population into the Assumption Monastery. We have limited food. His fiends scour the land watching and alerting him to anyone that dares go outside the walls. They rape and murder those they find, feeding on the corpses of the dead or hanging them as warning to others."

"It has been 150 years since such blasphemy has struck our beloved sacred homeland." Abbot Sylvester spoke. His words slow and pondered. His mouth nearly invisible behind a long thick white beard. He fondled the cross hanging from his neck as he stared blankly ahead in thought. "The great city of Novgorod has never recovered from the desecration and the sacking of the Oprichnina that followed. No one believes in devils any more, only traitors to the king. These spirits work through lies and manipulation. They use their million eyes to learn our strategy and use it against us. We must show Father Pyotr what he is up against and aid him all we can in dispelling this affront to the Holy Father from our country!"

They took Father Pyotr below the monastery to chambers used long ago to hold prisoners. They continued to the most solitary of these cells where several torches were lit within the circle of which hung a man of great stature. His clothes had once been quite regal and of a style popular centuries ago to Pyotr's eyes. They now were soiled and tattered. Mice ran about the room and scurried at the approach of the monks. The prisoner was chained to either wall by his hands, forced to stand eternally. He had five silver daggers thrust within his chest surrounding his heart and each of his eyes and his ears had golden crucifixes plunged within them. His mouth had been sewn shut. His hair grew long and thin behind him, trailing half way down his back.

"This is the demon Kazamir, whose affront against God is being paid by his imprisonment here."

"Why not kill him?"

"You cannot kill what is not alive. He will not cease to be a demon. We have failed to cast him back to hell. God has tasked us with keeping him here until He decides the time is right to deal with Kazamir Himself."

"What do the daggers do around his heart?"

"They prevent him from communicating back to Satan, his master. As long has the daggers are in place, his strength is less than that of aged man weak with disease."

"And the crucifixes?"

"Kazamir had many minions and that still exist. They see and hear for him. They do his bidding. But he is powerless to see through their eyes with the holy cross of Christ blinding him. He has no ability to hear with the blessed cross of Christ in his ears. We bind him here, we can do no more than this."

Kazamir let out a long snake-like laugh, breathing in heavily through his nose. He spoke arduously through his bound lips that had loosened over years of age in the twine. "I smell you priests before me. I can't hear or see you but I know you are there. I know why you are here for it is time for another to rise. I've counted the days through the smell of the air, the movements of the rats in my cage. I've waited, knowing what none of you had guessed. That I am but one of many. Not the first and not the last."

"Don't listen to his poison, we must reseal his lips. The abhorrence should not be allowed to speak to the living. His words are but an infection. Lie upon lie meant to deceive, drain hope and seduce the weak to his cause." Abbot Sylvester led the Fathers back up out of the dungeon as Kazamir hissed his laughter on behind them.

"Father Pyotr, I shall send Father Kliment and Father Leonid with you in a carriage with four horses. You must rush back with all speed to Tikhvin. Father Kliment will bring the daggers and crucifixes needed to bind the demon Vasily as well as blessed vessels on silver chains that must be dipped in holy water to be used to keep the minions of darkness at bay. They cannot come near you under the protection of God, remember that."

A small girl was heard desperately calling for help at the front gates of the monastery. Maxim was alerted and called out to her. "Who are you little girl and how did you make it here yourself?"

"I'm Kalia," She cried out, "my family tried to make it here but we were attacked. My papa told me to keep running to the monastery."

"I am sorry for your family Kalia, I am coming down to get you." Maxim lowered the rope ladder and climbed down for the little six year old girl with tattered clothes and dirty face to match her dirty blonde hair. She had tears streaming down her brown eyes. "There there little one, I've got you now, nothing more can happen to you. Climb on my back and hold on tight as I get us back up the ladder."

She did as she was told and Maxim began to climb, when Kalia took a poisoned pin she had in her hand and pushed it into Maxim's neck. He cried out and she jumped from him to land on her back and then turned to flee. Maxim's grip on the rope grew weak and he fell back to the grass. His vision blurred as hundreds of rats began to crawl over him. Above him a frantic attempt to save him began. They rushed to get holy water and toss it upon him, but before it could make its mark, the army of rats had begun carry him off away from the monastery towards the dark church of Vasily.

Maxim awoke in the hole in the midst of the desecrated church of the Blessed Trinity. The odor of guano was the first sense to return to him as he slowly opened his eyes to a world of ghastly madness. Countless bats hung far above him. Before him he heard the sounds of ritualized sex and sacrifice of animals and people. Oksana came down the rubble before him, undressed and with desire on her face. She opened his pants and began to rub on his cock until he could not help be but aroused by her. She climbed upon him and rode him, moaning her pleasure until she was satisfied and give him a single kiss on the lips before walking back up to the slaughter stones before him.

"Maxim my boy, so glad you could make time to continue our conversation." Maxim looked behind him to see Vasily on his charred throne. He pulled up his pants and rose to face the monster.

"What do you want from me, just kill me and be done with it you abomination to the Holy Father!"

"It's not what I want, its what you want that concerns me. I saw how you enjoyed Oksana. She enjoyed you as well. I cannot give her what she needs but you can. You are young and fertile. Stay here and we shall serve your every need and you will have your way with her at any time and any way you wish. You may have anyone else here if you choose as well, as long you give Oksana what she needs that is all we ask of you. We are but a band of hooligans and ruffians. Compared to my other male disciples you are a prince fit to birth a king. A child of yours who shall rule the world Maxim. Think of it! And all you have to do is fuck!"

Without a chance to answer, Maxim was dragged by men from the pit to lie across the bloodied stones. They pored a dark bitter drink down his throat which he wretched and fought against, but they beat him to accept it until he had downed it completely. Men and women removed his clothing and Oksana approached him once again, this time as a cat on all fours, her eyes full of seduction and desire as she lapped his limp penis into her mouth and began to gently work it across her tongue. The tonic took its affect and he felt intense desires for sexual dominance of her. He grabbed her by the hair and threw her down across the stone, her ass wiping slick against the thick coating of blood. He entered her, his emotions confused, his mind racing. He wanted to fight this urge but the compulsion was beyond him. He knew there was no future for him, death could only be the final outcome of this, but the mind altering powers of the drink and the wafting incense controlled his desires completely. He was at the mercy of his cock. He choked her, hating her, yet craving the feel of her. Slowly his hand went from her throat to her breast and he moaned from the euphoria of being inside her. All else

59

faded away and he gave way to his desires, exhaling all his devotion inside of her. Giving way to the call of his body and offering her all he had to give.

He sat upon her for a moment, still releasing his passion, breathing heavily to recover. Vasily stood before him and grabbed Maxim by the top of his head and ripped out his throat, throwing his choking gagging body into the pit where the dogs and rats leaped to feast as he slowly died. Vasily then mounted Oksana himself striking her firmly across the face to draw blood from her lip and nose. He pounded her endlessly upon the stone filling her with his monstrous juices and then lifting her by the arm to carry her where she would rest and conceive whatever depraved being was set to come of such as abominable union.

Father Nikita, who had been issued towards Saint Petersburg, had been attacked by dogs and found near death in Kirovsk. Only after a week of convalescence had he the strength to use a pen and write down what was happening in Tikhvin. This message had just reach Saint Petersburg as Pyotr and the carriage returned to town. As it neared the city, it was immediately besieged by the demons of Vasily. They had come armed for this and Pyotr swung a blessed vessel dipped in holy water on a chain about him leaning himself outside the carriage, clearing a path for their progress to continue to the Assumption Monastery. He knew if they approached the monastery by any of the direct paths the hellish followers of Vasily would bar their way and strike them down. He had a plan for this, taking the road behind the monastery towards the back entrance. He swung the amulet about him searching everywhere for rogues bent on waylaying them, the horses panting from the hard run. From the left someone fired a shot at them, which missed. The driver pushed the horses faster. They had little left to give. Before him he now saw the way blocked by a dozen men. He told the driver to continue right through them. Some of the men were armed and others held burning torches. They fired and struck the driver who fell from the carriage. As it passed the rogues, they threw their torches within and the carriage began to burn. Pyotr grabbed the bag of sacred artifacts from Novgorod and leaped across the top of the carriage and to the first horse. Father Kliment and Leonid leapt both aflame from the burning chariot and were slain mercilessly by the rogues. Pyotr brought the horses to a stop and worked to quickly free one of the two leads as the miscreants ran back towards where he had stopped. Leaping bareback upon this horse he raced it forward, leaning low to avoid the shots being fired behind him. The terrible bats swooped at him and the horse and he again began to swing the amulet to drive them away. From the side of the road came the terrible hell hounds to follow as close as the amulet allowed them. He was certain the back entrance would be heavily blocked to prevent him entrance but he intended to drive towards it until the last minute so they would not suspect his actual plan. He veered the horse suddenly to the Tikvinka river and pushed it to swim across. Several of the fiendish dogs swam after, keeping their distance from the spray of his amulet. More shots were fired at him and the horse panicked as it was hit. He pushed it on, flailing the amulet until he was struck in the shoulder and dropped it into the waters. He grabbed his bag from the horse and slid off to swim on his own. The bats were plummeting from above and the dogs were close behind him. He dove under and swam with all his might for the shore. As his hand finally found land, a dog grabbed him by his shoe and began ripping it apart in its powerful teeth. He pulled his foot from the shoe and lunged from the river upon the shore, bats lashing at his face and neck in such numbers he could not see where he was going. He reached into his bag and found the second amulet and began to swing it, once again clearing a path of twenty some feet around him. Beyond this barrier was darkness, a constant spinning wheeling mob of bats with at least five vicious dogs glaring at him from the periphery. He reached the underbrush beyond the river's edge and pressed his way through the foliage to the hidden tunnel opening there. He ran through this, flailing his protection about him and screaming ahead for someone to hear him and open the door. He pounded upon it, shouting for attention. The dogs, bats and rats keeping the barest distance they must from him. He saw men entering the far end of the tunnel and pounded harder begging for someone to hear his cries. At last, Father Semyon pried the door open and pulled him in, barring it quickly shut behind them.

Their secret passageway revealed, the monks were forced to break apart a section of inner wall within the monastery and use it to seal the tunnel from entry again. They worked on this tirelessly with the help of the men of Tikhvin, the sound of their enemies pounding on it from the other side driving them on.

The torches began their approach of the monastery two hours after sunset. A battalion of troops was on their way to Tikhvin though no one in the monastery knew of this. Vasily knew, for his spies roamed everywhere. He no longer had time to starve them out of their holy keep.

Stepan, a nobleman with military experience led the defense of the monastery. They had scant firearms, but they used these now on the approaching foes. The whirling storm of bats shielded their enemies from harm. The rogues lit the outer wooden doors on fire. The masons had sealed all the entrances to the monastery with stones, brick and mortar. As the great doors collapsed over in flames, the horde began assaulting these walls with pick axes. The bats could not fly so close to the walls of the sacred place and the bullets finally met their marks. Shouts rang out from within the monastery and Stepan could see a fire burning from the second gate. He issued half his armed men to defend the second gate, but they hadn't time to reach it before the brickwork gave way under canon fire. The fortifications were breached and the servants of hell streamed in. Outside the walls great clouds of bats swarmed up screeching and putting terror in the hearts of everyone inside the monastery. The wild dogs of hell howled above this noise, driving the frenzy up higher. Stepan rallied his men to repel the invaders and the blood of both sides began to spill freely on the sacred ground. Behind the fighting, more of Vasily's congregants came through the breach, dumping ash of the burnt corpses of children across the yard just inside the fallen gate fortification. Through the opening a stream of bats gushed in as a sudden flood. They wheeled about, confined to the circle of ash. Their impact on the morale of the townsfolk defending the monastery was devastating. Amidst this screeching frantic cloud Vasily entered, surrounded by hell hounds and thousands of scurrying rats that climbed up him, squealing, their darks eyes seemingly alight from the growing flames. The stench of burnt corpses and the thousands of rats filled the courtyard.

Father Trofim and four other monks including Pyotr chose to confront Vasily. Pyotr swung the sacred amulet about them as they approached. Father Semyon held the Mother of God icon aloft. Vasily simply smiled at them, dozens of rats climbing over him as he stood his ground.

Father Trofim stepped forward towards Vasily, "You have no place here servant of Satan. The power of God Almighty repels you from this sacred place."

"I serve no one. I am my own god, Father. I smell your faith, the stench of it. Your belief is not strong enough Father Trofim. I taste your doubt, your fear, just as I tasted the fear of Father Anatoly, Father Vyacheslav, Father Gennady, Father Evgeny —"

"Cease your harassment! In the name of Jesus Christ Lord of Lords I command you —" His words were cut short as the dogs lunged forward and pulled him down, ripping him apart. Father Semyon's legs gave way and Pyotr grabbed the Mother of God to keep it aloft. The bats immediately swarmed them as he dropped the amulet to save the icon. There was nothing but blackness about the remaining monks, some of whom screamed in terror for salvation.

In the midst of the consuming chaos a small frail figure worked its way forward, unharmed, diligently approaching the demon. The bats, the rats, the dogs, none dare touch the figure. It stood before Vasily, dwarfed by his height, but unbroken by his maddening terror. It was Valentina grandmother of Dafna and Pyotr. She stood before Vasily, a simple wooden cross in her hand, a hand that shook from infirmity not fear. Her faith was indomitable and she continued to approach him. He stretched out his arms and shouted obscenities at her, threatening to make her his personal bitch, to fuck on top of the Mother of God icon until her bones gave way. She heeded his venom not, holding her cross before him and praying quietly to herself through the cacophony of chthonic clamor. The rats scurried about her feet madly, but she worried not. Vasily started to back away from her and the swarm of bats fell to disarray. Pyotr could now see his grandmother, though blood coursed down his face into his eyes and his hands ached from holding the icon aloft, the blood from hundreds of bites and scratches making his grip slick and difficult. Father Semyon rose from the ground and took the icon back from the young monk. Valentina continued forward, her faith was a blinding glow to Vasily who began to falter in his step. She pressed the wooden cross against him, her eyes closed in prayer and he was powerless against her. Pyotr pulled the daggers he had received in Novgorod from his belt and shoved one into Vasily's chest beside his heart. The demon screamed and collapsed to the ground, his night minions screamed in disarray, attacking Pyotr, but he no longer needed his eyes for his work and allowed them to ply their worst against him. Pyotr drove the remaining four daggers around the heart of the monster. Vasily lay still, unable to raise himself. Pyotr with drew the four crucifixes and pressed the first threw the left eye of Vasily, gore bursting out as he pierced the eyeball and pressed it deep within. He continued this with the second eye and then both ears, and a deafening silence enveloped the night.

Part IV

The Apostle Peter

Abrafo stood amidst the downpour at the shore, waves crashing against the beach, the spray of saltwater stinging his eyes. The distant strikes of lightning showcasing the ship he had foreseen battling the chaotic seas and driven dangerously towards the shore. Its rudder lost, masts torn and broken, the ship's fate was sealed. With the next series of flashes, Abrafo could see the ship collapsed on its side, slowing falling prey to the great mouth of the deep.

By morning the cargo he anticipated washed ashore. He approached the wooden crate with a mix of fear and excitement.

Abrafo was 16 when his family was taken from him by slavers. His mother heard their approach and told him to run as fast as he could to the woods. He obeyed her. He waited for hours until it grew dark and then crept back to his house. No one was there and no one would ever return. The elderly in the village were crying for their losses. Besides the infants and small children, he was the youngest left. They told him it was now up to him. He had to stand up and be not just a man, but the man for his village for they had no one else. Abrafo was terrified and ran from his village, tears streaming from him, calling out for his mother. He stopped at the edge of a stream and stared down at his reflection in the water, his face strained with anger and pain. He picked up a stick and lashed out at his image crying with each strike, shuddering with gasping moans of despair. He dropped the stick in the water and it slowly drifted away. He watched as it went, sitting down on the bank and placing his head upon his knees. He was not ready to be a man, much less the only man in his village. He was too weak. He was a thin boy never growing much muscles. He had always been picked on by the other children for being too slow, not being able to keep up, couldn't climb the but the easiest of trees.

A beetle suddenly hovered in the air before him, large and gorgeously iridescent. It looked straight at him as it hovered less than a foot away. He reached out his hand and it landed in his palm. He drew it to him, admiring the beauty and the fathomless dark of its eyes. He felt a pull from those eyes as if they were calling him to drop deeper and deeper within them. He yielded himself to this and his being left his body. He saw his mother locked in a cell with other women wailing and striking themselves. He saw his father in yet another cell with many more men. He sat upon the ground staring before his feet, tears streaming from an emotionless face. He saw himself freeing his parents and all the prisoners, bringing them back to the village where a huge celebration was made in his honor with singing and dancing and a great feast.

Abrafo did not return to his village. He followed the visions of the beetle far from his home towards the coast. Not where his parents were held, but where the shipwreck was set to take place.

He approached the wooden cargo box that had washed ashore. It was damaged on one side so he climbed up and worked at this point, struggling, but making slow progress with freeing the nails. Over time he made enough room to slip inside. In the dark of the container he saw layers of wet straw, slick stones, a bag which when touched was filled with long metal pieces with strange sharp ends. Then he heard a moan and with a fright he turned to see a white woman with long dark hair, bleeding from her face, nearly drowned and heavily pregnant. He ran back and fought further with the opening he had begun, trying some of the strange tools in the bag to help his progress. The side fell away and light shown in. He grabbed the woman by her arms and pulled her out to the sand, but she was already dead. He slapped her to revive her, but she poured nothing but seawater from her mouth. He pushed her to her side to pour this water out and slapped her some more asking her to wake up. After time he gave up and sat despondent, feeling he had failed. Surely his mission had been to save this woman. Then a thought entered his mind. Perhaps the baby was not dead. He felt her extended belly and sensed there was still a warmth there. Taking one of the curious blades he carefully sliced her open. She made no reaction and he cried from the horrific effort of it, but kept on until the womb was fully exposed. Reaching in he felt it and a small hand reached back to him through the womb. He carefully cut the womb open and pulled the child out. He cried out his joy and named the child Iniko.

He buried the dead woman in the sand and took the bag of blades. Rigged some ropes he tied them to the stones and drag them behind him. He also made a makeshift björn for Iniko. The stones were extremely light, almost weighing nothing to him. He bore these goods and the child back to the jungle, back to a place the beetle specified to him where several red boulders lay and placed the stones before them. Abrafo then returned to his village bearing the child and left Iniko with the old women to care for as he went back to save his parents. They said he was foolish, they were lost and he should stay with them, stay with the living who needed him. But his mind was settled, he was certain he would succeed.

The beetle continued its visions to Abrafo, showing him how to make a special fire with an enchanting smell to its smoke and a variety of dark drinks that produced further visions and sensations, many of which Abrafo had never experienced at his age. And then the beetle showed him how to take something that was alive and make it not alive. He started with a frog, which Abrafo was adept at catching in great numbers. Once the sacrament was complete and the frog came back, Abrafo pushed away in amazement. The next familiar would be something much more dangerous. Something that could help bring his parents back and make him a hero in his village.

Abrafo sat outside the slave prison in Douala waiting for a sign. It was deep in the night, clouds covered a nearly full moon. He believed his parents had not been shipped off yet. He believed what the scarab had promised him. The screams began to issue from within the prison. A light rain pelted down upon him and he pressed his face up to it. More screams as his black mamba made its rounds of the guards, striking at will. The front door flew open and a man fell convulsing to the ground. Abrafo ran to him and rolled him over to reveal the keys he had. Taking these he rushed into the prison and began opening all the doors, calling for everyone to run for their lives. The prisoners ran as he opened cage door after cage door but he did not see or hear his mother or father. He prayed he had just missed them in the flurry of desperate bodies rushing and crashing into him, crying and fleeing with measureless desperation to get back to their home and loved ones. Abrafo ran with them as more guards were alerted to the chaos at the slave prison and shots rang out against the fleeing escapees. He felt alive. He felt powerful. He felt he had found his purpose in life. No longer the weak Abrafo, but Abrafo the strong. Abrafo the brave. Abrafo the powerful.

He had not rescued his parents. He had not rescued anyone from the village. They had all been shipped off long before he'd arrived. There was no celebration, no glory, but the beetle promised him power nonetheless. Its eyes showed him riches, women, spectacular sensations of pleasure. It lured him with these visions. It promised him everlasting life and dominance over all his enemies. He followed the beetles visions. It taught him to make potions and elixirs that brought him deeper insight – insight into himself and into the mystical realm the creature was leading him into. Abrafo surrounded himself with familiars to guard and protect him. He became known as the sorcerer-child and many avoided him while others came to see and learn. As Iniko grew, he joined him and Abrafo taught him many of the same skills the beetle had shown to him. Over time his followers multiplied and he nourished them on potions and fragrant incense that lit passionate unbridled desires and led to manic desperate orgies. The years spun on, he aged slowly unlike the others. The beetle kept him instilled with elixirs that unbound him from his earthly body to see far into the future; the inevitabilities that were to come and the part he had to play in them.

Iniko led the raiding parties into neighboring villages for livestock and victims of their gruesome sacrifices and brutal orgies. Abrafo focused on seclusion and avoiding undo attention of the outside world. He did not want to risk warfare with his Animist and Islamic neighbors. As the Moslem increased in power in the area, he grew more concerned and counseled Iniko to be careful what attention he draws to their community. But Iniko's blood-lust grew with his age. Whether his sire was Maxim or Vasily was uncertain, but he had a fire in his heart that demanded action. Iniko guarded himself with familiars including crows, jackals and a spider monkey named Cashile. They took other cult members with them on hunts of the villages that surrounded them. On such a raid they were preparing to attack some women washing clothes at a stream when Iniko saw the most beautiful sight his eyes had ever beheld. Her name was Shani and she waded topless out of the stream bearing a basket of clothing on her. He was mesmerized by her. He had no feelings to own or demand she pleasure him. He wanted nothing more than to look at her. She smiled and laughed to one of the other women and he was completely taken by her. He ordered his men back and he stayed by the river. He sent his crows out to follow her and learn where she lived.

Iniko watched her from the forest at her home village the next day as she conversed with her family and spoke with friends. It was not a way of living he was familiar with, but her spirit drew him to it. He suddenly felt confused by his life and he ran off far from everyone to contemplate his feelings alone. Only Cashile followed him and when Iniko saw this he rebuked her and sent her back away. He spent six days alone with his thoughts and then came back to Abrafo.

"My good friend, you brought me into this life and gave me all that I have. I owe everything to you and I can never repay this debt."

"Iniko, there is no debt to me that you owe."

"Then I ask you, only father I have ever known, will you allow me to leave our village, for I no longer feel I belong here. I've seen things that draw me to another way of life. The taste for blood and conquest has left my mouth sour. I have drunk of a sweetness that I never knew existed and it will never leave my thoughts now."

Abrafo thought on this. He wondered if allowing Iniko to leave was against the will of the spirit being in the beetle. "I will have to consult on this Iniko. Please allow me until the morning to give you my answer."

Iniko was pleased that Abrafo was not angry with him. He set back into the forest to scream his joy and think about the life he would soon have with Shani.

Abrafo allowed Iniko to leave. His visions that night showed him this course was inevitable and necessary towards the destiny yet to come. Iniko thanked Abrafo for his mercy. Abrafo provided Iniko with goods, supplies and riches so that he may make an impression on the father of Shani. Iniko set off for Shani's village. Cashile followed and he sent her away, he wanted no part of his old life to follow him.

Iniko reached her village and presented his gifts to Shani's father and the chief of village requesting to wed Shani. There was much discussion by the village elders, some feared he was one of the devils from the forest cult. They allowed him to live with them to decide his honesty in this pursuit. Iniko accepted this role with complete dedication and earned the respect of the entire village. He was allowed to wed Shani and his heart burst with joy. Their wedding night was the most glorious and passionate love making he had imagined. Without the fire of the intoxicants and the fever of the incense, it was nothing but the union of two souls in care and desire for one another. They lay in each others arms aware of the other's heartbeat. Feeling a peace that transcended explanation. Iniko knew this was where he belonged, this was what the course of his life should look like and he faded to sleep with the prize of his life warmly wrapped within his arms.

Shani woke to find Iniko cold, his arms still around her. She screamed for help and continued screaming in her terror and grief. The elders assembled and examined his corpse. He had been stabbed in the night with a thorn dipped in poison. Only something small and silent could have entered without notice and performed this murder.

Abrafo saw the crows and the jackals fall dead and he knew that Iniko was no more. He cried for this and wondered what he had done wrong, his vision had shown this was the path that must be taken. It took him years to understand that Cashile had performed the murder and had died herself from it. The monkey had a mind beyond that of the other familiars and once Iniko had completed the task required of him, she took her retribution on his betrayal.

Shani bore a son from her union with Iniko and raised him as Ngozi. The tribe she belonged to was raided by Moslems and the survivors chose to convert. Through time Ngozi's heirs rose in importance as the Fulani took hold of the region leading to the greatest of his descendants, Adama.

When Abrafo had reached 135 years of age, he knew the culmination of his wait was reaching its conclusion. The Fulani, under Adama, launched a jihad against Abrafo and destroyed everything within miles of his forest sanctuary. His followers were either slaughtered or sold into slavery. But Abrafo had known of their coming for a very long time and returned only once it was safe for him to do so. Everything the beetle had told him had come to pass. He had only to wait for the Moslem trader who dared to tread through this desolated land.

Part V

Kazamir

Archbishop Pimen sat staring out the window of the Yuriev Monastery at the rolling dark balls of smoke that belched up from the surrounding countryside. The monastery was surrounded by chaos, evil of the highest order, and he felt powerless against it. The demon and his multitude continued to lay waste to all of Novgorod and he had no way of stopping it. His face, emotionless yet bound by two lines of flowing tears as he prayed constantly for guidance against this darkness that struck irrepressibly across all that lay before him. Flocks of crows billowed into the sky, minions and spies for the monster. Dozens of his countrymen had been seduced to join the devil and rampaged the city and countryside; lust for blood, sex and torture ravaging their once Christian souls. He wavered in his hold of the window and Father Fadey caught him, dampening his brow, bringing him away from the window to rest on a chair.

"Where have I failed my God?" Cried out Pimen.

"You have been a faithful servant, this is but a test and one you shall overcome."

"It is lost, he is bound to take all of Novgorod within days. There are no forces left to place against him."

"Holy Father, you know that is not true, God's will always provide a way."

Archbishop Pimen grabbed Father Fadey by the arm tightly. "We must bring anyone we can into the monastery. They will be lost if we don't. Send out word, bring all food supplies we can, this will be our last holdout I can feel it."

Father Fadey rushed with the order.

The street smelled of piss and rot. It soaked the stones and filled the cracks. Leaves sailed across it as tiny majestic boats while insects and rats scurried in search of anything dying or near death. Alla was pissing, providing an energetic push to the pale little leaf she had kept her eye on. It spun away from her further down the dark alley, soon to be crushed by the shoes of some passer-by or a horse bearing a load of hay.

In her hand she held one of the delicate wooden deer her sweet brother had carved for her. She caressed it tenderly, following the lines of his carving and kissing it on its forehead between the two fragile horns. Her brother Ilia returned, swinging wildly upside down with his ankles held from above by a heavy set man. Dropping Ilia upon his head, the man removed a flask from his vast warm coat and poured the liquid like water down his throat. The empty container shattered beside

Alla sending shards against her and she shielded her eyes from it. He grabbed her by her arm and swung her over his shoulder, turning to part from the alley that had been her home for the past few months. Ilia stumbled after them. She could see blood running down his head across his beat red cheeks. His cheeks always turned red when he was angry. And he always cried as he was doing now. He was six, and small for six. She was nine and she was beautiful. And that was why this was happening.

Ilia begged and pleaded for the release of his sister, but Iakov plod on, towards his mansion ignoring the brat, his hungry degenerate urges already hot at the thought of stripping the girl of her rags. Iakov had seen the boy scurrying about the market for weeks when he spied the young angel standing silent off in a shadowed alleyway. His heart pained to own her on sight, such sad beauty shining through layers of caked mud and filth. A piercing set of eyes that wounded him with a desire he could not – would not control. To feel her now under his grasp. She didn't struggle against him. She simply watched her brother pleading for her release. His wife was off to see her mother. When she'd return, he'd introduce the child as a new servant. But tonight was all that mattered right now. Tonight his every fantasy was to be fulfilled.

The guard at the front door picked up Ilia by the neck and genitals and tossed him from the mansion back onto the street. The last she saw was her sweet brother being kicked in the ass and screaming more from failing her than his physical pain. The door closed behind her and Iakov was now her master. She thought of her parents, uncle, aunt, cousins all lost to the plague that went as quickly as it had come, leaving only Ilia and her to fend for themselves in the strange world left behind. She thought of her mother mostly. She thought of her kindness, How she washed her, the wonderful foods she would make. The stories she told her at bedtime. How she let them play when daddy would have said to be quiet. She thought of mama's garden filled with magical things that tasted so good. She thought of mama's arms around her singing to her. The feel of her fingers as Alla ran her tiny hand across them. "Mamma!" She cried out as Iakov thrust himself within her, the pain as if she were breaking open, his hot sweaty body pressing down making breath unachievable. She held to mamma's gentle songs as the remnants of childhood were torn from her.

Timor was singing one of his drunken songs again as the other children tended the fire and chewed on the few scraps left of their pitiful rations. Ilia could see Timor rubbing the flask in his pocket. The one Ilia had given him earlier that day when you presented his plot to rob Iakov. Timor's crew of child thieves were small time, not up to such a dangerous endeavor, but Ilia had spent significant time crafting his words, devising a fool proof plan. He'd watched the movements of the mansion where his darling Alla was held. He knew the breath of the building, how it woke and how it slept. He'd been supplying the guard with a watered down vodka for months in exchange for scraps from the evening meal. Tonight, the vodka was full strength and the guard would be out within the hour. He knew where the key was. He knew where Alla slept at night. And he knew where the accursed Iakov lay snoring in his personal stench.

Ilia, Timor and four of the best thieves approached the manor. Ilia ran ahead and carefully took the key from the slumbering guard. They followed him as he opened the door and the crew crept within.

"Vasha and Sergey, go to the kitchen and collect the best food and anything we can sell." Timor instructed. Ilia didn't wait for instructions and went straight for the master's bedroom. He could hear the monster's taxed breathing as he approached the door. Ilia timed the opening of the door with Iakov's creaking inhalation and the dim light poured down upon the mountainous lard of the man, heaving and gasping for breath as it slept. Ilia crept towards the bed carefully reviewing his surroundings. He'd waited three years for this and nothing was going to chance. He could smell the monster now. Ilia was shaking and bit his tongue to calm himself, reaching into his pocket as he'd practice for the blade — it wasn't there! A moment of absolute panic ensued. How did this happen? He felt flush, blood pumping into his head. Ilia held his breath and closed his eyes to focus his attention — focus his hatred. He took seven deep breaths still with his eyes closed and then opened them. On the table besides the bed was a scissors. With infinite calm he picked this up in is hand and approached the mass of fat and blood that he intended to conquer. A final deep peaceful inhalation accompanied by complete emptiness and calm as he left his body and took his mind back to the fields near the childhood home where he would chase his friends and hear the cries of his sister that she wasn't being included in the games. No one wanted a little girl to play, even if she was his sister and she was crying. Iakov's hands grabbed at Ilia's face, but he'd expected this and bent back, plunging the blades deep into the neck and pressing together with all his young might willing the pair to join again. His muscles ached from the strain. Iakov gouged at Ilia's eyes, gurgling a desperate muted plead for help. The smell of blood and an unexpected blast of gas and feces as the panic man succumbed to his earned misfortune. Ilia sat for an unknown time upon the warm bleeding corpse, his tense hands still clenched around the weapon fully closed now within his victim's neck, unable to let go, unable to open his eyes. The hate remained. He new Iakov was dead, but the hate remained. It wasn't enough to kill him. With this realization tears streamed unbidden down his face. He clenched to stop them, but it was no use. He began to sob opening, drool running down his chin. He couldn't take it back. All the suffering of his family, his parents, his sister, himself — none of it was paid for by the death of this scourge and Ilia's pain freed itself from the bonds he had held it in check with. He fell from the bed to the wet bloody floor and shook with silent sobs. At the door, though he knew it not, stood Timor in shock at the sight. Alla's hand was clenched in his and he unknowing tighten it as he looked upon the gore and horror of the room. Alla stood emotionless, the pain of Timor's firm clench was soothing to her. She was used to pain in this house. To have it end abruptly before she had left might have driven her mad. She needed to see the fat man bleed and the uncompromising love of a younger brother willing to give everything for her safety.

Ilia was catatonic for days following the robbery. Alla tended to her beloved brother, covering him with her kisses and holding him in her arms to the songs of their innocence. With all this affection, Ilia's dreams were of pure nightmare. Everything he touched turned to death. Death collected about him, drawn to him, surrounding him to protect him from anything good. Death became his only companion, his only purpose and slowly his only pleasure.

Ilia awoke straining to press the scissors together through the thick gushing neck of Iakov, his own dry throat crying out with hatred and agony. Then silence. He was unfamiliar with the room he was in. It was nice. It reminded him of Iakov's bedroom, but it was different. His head was bursting, the blood felt like it would flood out upon the blanket he was cocooned within. The blanket was wet where he'd pissed himself recently, but no it was cum. He jumped from the bed, falling on his weak legs and striking his head to the wooden floor. He pressed his forehead against its coldness and breathed.

The hallway led him, even before he heard the sounds. Each forward step came unbidden as he was pulled towards his destiny. The sounds began, though he blocked them out initially, willing them not to be. They grew as he approached their genesis. His heartbeat burned with its forceful pounding. His knees weakened but his hand still grabbed the doorknob. He opened it and let the revelation take hold of him. There was not overwhelming emotion. They all coursed across him evenly, erratically leaving him confused, unstable, wanting to react but nailed where he stood, his eyes pealed open to watch. Timor fucked Alla with a frenzy of one consumed by the single thing worth living for. One demon for another. Ilia went for Timor's satchel which lay beside the bed, pulling out the blade the master of thieves kept at ready and lunged across the bed bent on slicing open the pulsing sack hanging between Timor's legs. The thrust missed its mark and he stabbed his master in the ass, Timor pivoting off his sister to strike Ilia with all his might across his right cheek. Ilia fell from the bed, his vision momentarily abandoning him. Timor wrenched the blade free and picked the boy up to throw him against the far wall of the room screaming expletives and promises of unimaginable pain. Soon the other street urchins surrounded Ilia kicking and punching and cursing him until his small battered form could take no more.

The prison cell felt right. The momentary existence in the warm house Timor has acquired with Iakov's wealth was all wrong. Comfort was for the past, when his family was still intact. Here he could think. Here he could feel. Feel the hatred, the anger, the desperation to save the only person who meant anything to him. Ilia punished himself with what she must be going through, how his efforts to save her simply made her life worse. Now that Timor had him jailed for assault he was impotent to save her. Yes, it felt right to be here. Amidst the dredge of society. Buried in the depths of the city, below the filth, below the shit, where his screams would be meaningless, answered only by laughter, the scurry of insects, the inattention of rats. The pleasure of the guards who took their turns with the beautiful pale boy who no longer gave a fight to their advances having succumbed to his fate as a toy for the depraved.

Three years past in that cell below the city, a crypt for his body and soul. Three years his body was ravaged by guards, monks and high paying noblemen hungry to lick and suck about the stem of such a sweet hairless penis and feel the firm young ass of a gorgeous boy. Each of them burning with desire, wanting for just a moment to own something so beautiful, so pure so young and clean. They would take him out of the dungeon to the upper levels of the monastery where he would be washed and dressed in silks, brushed with perfumed powders, massaged with sensual oils. Some nights they would bring crowds from out of town; countless hands grabbing at him, teethmarks on his chest and neck, his anus sore and burning, his stomach full from the flows of semen thrust eagerly down his throat.

After three years of such abuse, allowing his whole being to be used for but the pleasure of men's aching fevered greed, Ilia lay amidst the hairy stink of four noblemen. The night was hot and the window was open. Gently his pulled himself from beneath their sweaty lustful embrace and tipped carefully from the bed, robing himself in the garments they had provided him, as ill-purposed as they were for his ambition. Deftly he worked through their clothes and satchels collecting a considerable sum to get him started. He slipped out the window and crawled down the rocky wall, his fingers and toes torn and bleeding from the effort to find grip. He made his way to the ground and momentarily froze in the shadows. The sleeping city lay before him. A sight forbidden of him for three years yet immediately so familiar and unchanged. He was shaking. She was out there. And so was Timor.

Three days and nights Ilia hid across from the house that Timor had purchased with Iakov's wealth. He watched the cadre of child thieves enter and vacate the building. Some were familiar, many were fresh-faced. There was

74

a constant stream of new blood available in Novgorod for Timor and his ilk. Children with nowhere else to turn. Boys who would die if they didn't turn to a life of petty theft or worse. Alla was in there. He'd seen her return once. He must have dozed off when she left, but she came back with bread and fish. She was feeding the monster. All Ilia could think of was killing Timor. There was no easy way to do it. The best chance he had was when the devil slept. He'd purchased the perfect blade in the market and worked to sharpen it as he waited and watched for his opportunity.

"Ilia," the gentle voice tugged at him as he slept. His mind crept back to childhood beside the fireplace playing with wooden toys carved by their father with Alla as mother filled the home with the warm smell of dinner. "Wake up my sweet." Slowly he roused himself from his slumber to find his precious sister above him smiling warmly upon him like a glow from heaven.

"Alla?"

She laughed, "Yes my love." and he burst into her arms kissing her endlessly, streams of tears flowing warmly across his cheeks and he shuddered in utter joy.

"I've missed you so much, my Alla." His words came amidst spasms of cries of near despair mixed with joy and unexpected pleasure. She was here. She was safe. He could feel her. He could smell her. It was her eyes, her smile. He touched her face, pulled her to him and wept relentlessly wishing this was real but certain it was but a dream.

She shushed him, bidding him to take a drink to relax, and laid him in her lap as he quivered in pain, joy and confusion holding her hand as so tightly within his two it hurt her but she dare not complain. All he could do was repeat her name amidst his cascade of tears, his mouth drooling though he did not know it. He was overwhelmed. It was far too much for him to take for her to actually be here after all he had prayed, worked and fought for. Her name, he repeated like a mantra, the only comfort left in his world, the only reason he fought to stay alive amidst the madness. Her tears fell upon him as she caressed his head and he slowly quieted. The shuddering calmed, but the tears still poured forth. He loved her for all that she was. He loved her for she was goodness. She was sacred. She was precious and worth dying for. She was God and Goddess in one. She was his sister and he was her brother. They were family and nothing could break that love.

All that followed was rumor to him. He was present and not present for it. Her words, biblical, drove him unthinking toward her charge of him. He knew not when she left him or if he left her. He felt no passage of time, no movement, no change of scenery. He would never speak to her or feel her touch again. She had protected him from certain death for Timor knew Ilia was hunting him. The ruse of movement outside the house was a ploy but to draw him out, to seal a fate before he could even see his beloved sister again. It was her own guile that had saved him, her knowledge of her sweet brother that led her to find him first and protect him from the fates laid against him. For Timor lusted for Ilia's blood as much as Ilia ached for the blood of Timor. Two locked together in mutual hate over the same woman not yet woman. It was only Alla that could prevent this bloodshed. Only Alla could save the one in the world she truly cared for. Alla for Ilia, giving herself for him in the only way she could — with all that she had of herself to offer.

Her trust in Bogdan was misplaced. The kindness she saw in his eyes was but one of countless lies Bogdan had learned to craft through years of survival in this most wretched of lives he found himself fighting through. His wife, less than a degenerate whore. His children, ungrateful cunts each of them. But he had one secret on everyone — he knew a way out. He knew a way to change his fate and this boy, this wretch of a boy would be his salvation. For there were pleasures he had seen beyond that of dreams. He had only been allowed a sip with his eyes, but it was more than he needed. The desire consumed him, he knew there was something far beyond what had been offered him ever before if he had but the will to work for it. And he did. His lies were crafted with the deepest of deceit. Mercy was left far in his past. Desire for what was owed him, this is what fed his movements, his decisions, his every waking thought. Bogdan hammered Ilia against the cross in the Unnamable Field, pounding the nails into the young boys palms, watching the blood seep from the thorned cross he'd placed upon his head. He wrapped the boys genitals in a second twine of thorns, pulling the small penis tight against the boy's belly, dripping with fresh blood as the thorns dug deep. He took the ochre paste and plied it upon the end of his staff, pushing it into the young lad's mouth and twisting to make sure he sucked upon the mash. He lit the torches in a circle around Ilia and left the boy to the dark of night as the forces of deepest evil assembled for their vigil.

Ilia awoke to find himself nailed to Bogdan's cross. He wasn't sure if Alla had been a dream or if this was. Perhaps they both were. Perhaps he was still in prison being fucked by fat men at this very moment. The slight wind whipped amidst the torches and the pain of the thorns stabbing into his genitals made him cognizant of this reality. He breathed in a whimper at this, feeling like he might cry out of pity for himself. The thunder of hundreds of crows wings swarmed about him and took this breath away. He gaped into the dark at the fury of their swirling maddening rush. Their wings and eyes flickered in the light of the torches. He closed his eyes and strained away from them, feeling their rush against his skin and then silence. He breathed again and look out to the darkness. They were gone, but he was not alone. Amidst the torches he could see the eyes of dogs staring at him in the dimness. Their silence far worse than if they were howling.

His heart pounded, he strained against the nails pounded into his hands. He began to cry and peed upon himself, his upturned penis splashing it against his belly warmly. His knees weakened bring more pain to his palms and he slowly lost consciousness.

When he came to again, a young girl was pressing salves into his wounds gently. A fire was lit near him and the walls were of animal hide. He was in some sort of temporary structure. The girl was young, just older than him. Naked but for a necklace of bear claws, she massaged his wounded hands. He stared at her young breasts, just blooming, pink and attractive to him. She coaxed him to drink of the bitter she pressed to his lips. He took it down. She kissed him. He didn't return it. She lay down against him. He turned from her. Her breath felt sweet against his neck. He fell back into darkness.

Zoya was part of the People Apart, a small society that rejected the drive towards modernity, cities, empires that drove the world. Their life spoke of simplicity, nature, devotion to each other and rejection of the material. They lived on the move, rejected by the world just as they rejected it. They learned to keep their distance and be wary of strangers. Ilia healed in their camp and thought heavily on his fate. Had his sister betrayed him or had that all been a dream? Surely she still suffered in the grip of Timor. He had to free her. If but his last action, he wanted peace for his beloved.

Zoya and her people gave him nothing but tenderness and affection. Yet years of abuse by those that wanted something from him honed his instincts. Ilia knew they wanted something of him. What it was eluded him, but they wanted it with desperation. He was tired of giving of himself for the pleasure and gain of others. He knew his sister was out there. He knew she needed him. Nothing else mattered. Not his safety, not his happiness. He owed it to her to give all he could to free her from Timor. If he died trying, so be it. Alla was his family and he loved her with all his heart. Each night he was left to himself with a dog guarding his tent. This night he opened the flap to the tent and approached the mutt. It stared blankly back at him. He kneeled before it staring into its blank eyes. The mutt stared back at him, its breath, if anything, steady. Ilia grabbed it by the throat with both hands and clenched with all his might. The dog gave no struggle, watching with black lifeless eyes. He pressed it to the earth and pushed with his weight down on its neck. Slowly, the beast drooled, let forth a cough, pushing with its leg against him, its claws scraping his side and slowly it subsided to absolute silence. He maintained his grip, pushing it down to the earth until he was certain it had stopped breathing. And then he ran. Ran with all his might away from the camp into the darkness, into the unknown, back to his sister. Wherever she may be, he was coming. He would save her. They would be together again happy as before.

It was hours down the road when he heard the wailing of the child. The plea was weak and tired, having gone unsettled for some time. Ilia crept carefully as the sound grew closer. A wagon and horse stood before him, shadowed in the dark of night. He rounded the beast and glanced within the simple wagon where a swaddled newborn fought exhaustion to press forth another wail for succor. Off in the forest he heard a familiar sound. A sound that drew the blade into his had thoughtlessly. A sound that expelled emotion from him, eliminating all feeling and filling the void with calm determination. The fall of his footsteps. The beat of his heart. The quiet of the the forest. The thrusts and moans of the rapist. He closed his eyes and followed the sound only with his ears. Its familiarity a burden, yet a guide. Ilia felt a peace, a warmth as he grew closer. The rustle of leaves, the panting, the pressure to hold down the victim of the abuse. He followed the moan of a man taking what he wanted from another as had been done to him so many times. As was being done to his sister even now. With infinite calm and a sighing breath he sliced the man's throat clean, exhaling slowly as the form gurgled and convulsed before him. He fell to his knees in a ecstasy of accomplishment, the warm wet knife sinking from his fingers. He fell forward to the earth. This was done. This was practice. Timor was next.

The sun was pressing through the leaves above. He was on the wagon. The babe asleep was nestled against him tenderly. The horse was driven by a girl, her beauty unmistakable from behind. Her posture was pure poetry of feminine form, both strong and sensual. Dark hair cascaded across her shoulders. She led the horse with conviction and kindness. She knew he had stirred and his heart felt weak when she glanced with a smile in her gorgeous brown eyes at him, holding her gaze for an eternal moment before turning back to the road ahead.

She was Sofia and he had saved her. They returned to her home where she fed him, washed him, lay with him and sang to him. They never spoke a word to each other. She brought the baby girl to lay between them and she fed the child while she caressed his face. When the child drifted to sleep he made love to her, feeling for the first time the righteousness of such physical attention. She warmed him. Her softness felt so right. So young and generous. None of the stench of age and foul breath or the pain being beaten, gagged and the sore of countless penetrations. This was gentleness, mutual, harmony.

For the second time in his life he had a home. He had happiness. Sofia had laughter and joy always in her eyes. When she went about chores in her dress, the practice was a dance of infinite beauty that captivated Ilia until she chastised him for staring and neglecting his own work. Her kisses would come from nowhere when he least expected it. Tenderness that held him in the sweetest bondage to her. She owned him completely and there was no world outside of her.

He gathered wood for the coming winter. Hunted small game and trekked to the nearest lake to fish for their supper. As he returned with the setting of the sun, a change in mood within the house pressed against his progress. There was a pack propped near the front door. The smoke spoke of a larger fire than she usually would set and bellows, bellows of great laughter came muffled across the wind.

Thoughtlessly he dropped the fish, rabbit and the pack of wood on his back and crept silently to his home. His heart pounding. At the back of the house where he approached he found his things. Clothing, tools even the small toy reindeer he'd carved for baby Dina, all placed in bag along with some food supplies. He collapsed to the ground. Breathing grew difficult. Tears welled up and he felt he might burst outright, but held himself in check. The sound of the beast of a man now in his house. The father of her infant, long lost and thought dead. A sudden return after nearly a year afield.

Ilia sat there motionless for some time. Listening to the muffled laughter, the sounds of dinner, the heavy footfall of a large man confident in the home he'd built with his own hands, unaware of the young intruder who'd cared for and devoted himself completely to his wife for the past few months. Ilia brooded in his thoughts, shifting from flight to fight in countless variation, swirling currents of confliction burdening his young heart. Was she better off now? Was he good enough for her? Could this brute love her with a fraction of the dedication he held for her? Through the silence he heard an uninvited sound. He wished it away but was held like stone in its sway. She moaned beneath him. It started subtle, but became more desperate, hungry almost ravenous. Like a hound denied food for weeks finally given a fresh steak. She called the name of her husband again and again, pleading for him to own her completely, to ride her ruthlessly to his satisfaction. Illia heard the echoing cries as he satisfies his pent up craves for her and she poured forth all of her body for her beloved's pleasure.

He ran, ran with all his might. He took nothing with him, not even giving a thought to any action but to get away from the sounds that would haunt him forever.

He sat silently in the closet, hidden behind clothes and boots watching as his sister braided her long hair. Ilia held his knife firm and at the ready. He didn't greet his sister though he shared space with her after so much work to arrive here. She went to and from the room over the next few hours as the light settled into its western rest. He shifted his weight at times but was careful to avoid any noise. Then the moment arrived. He heard Timor's voice climbing the stairs. Alla had prepared candles in the bedroom and the dim shimmering light reflected the quiet rising of Ilia's heartbeat. His legs clenched to spring the moment opportunity presented itself. The footfalls approached, Timor was singing a silly nursery song in his crass voice, years of alcohol and tobacco leaving their mark. The steps stopped short of the room and Ilia held his breath willing his eyes to see through the wall at his prey. Into the room tumbled a small boy, instantly scooped up into Alla's arms and swung into the air to coos of delight. She covered the babe in her kisses and squeezed him against her. Ilia turned to stone, his shock only conquered by the unimaginable when she rushed herself into Timor's arms to kiss the rogue who picked the two up to dance them about the room in his arms. The three toppled upon the bed to tender words, affectionate kisses and endless attention to the toddler.

Ilia was no more. His every purpose in life now lay defeated. The night moved forward in a fog as he neither thought or felt anything but loss and desperation. He fled the house through his entry in the early hours when he knew Timor slept deepest. He stole a horse at the edge of town and road away. He no longer had tears to shed for himself or those he'd lost. He felt he'd never cry again. He knew he'd never love again. Not the love of family or the love of a woman. He rode back toward the camp of the People Apart reaching it after nightfall. Dropping from his horse he search for Zoya and when he found her, stood wordlessly before her. She stared back at him, unspeaking, unemotive. He dropped heavily to his knees before her and buried his face in the softness between her legs. She ran her fingers through his hair and he kissed her thighs and pussy endlessly. Thankful for something in this world that would accept him.

Ilia took a new name for himself, Kazamir. Over a decade on and Kazamir stood rugged, strong and lord over a brutal army. He gave up his heart for his fist. He traded his soul for a sword. He stood before a fire flickering in the night wind as he looked at the lights of Novgorod his childhood home and his next claim. Only Sophia's home and the manor of Timor were to be spared, all else he allowed fare game. He kept his thoughts from lingering on Alla and Sonia. He wasn't that boy any more. He would keep them safe, but they were his past, he would not seek them out for there was nothing to be gained but pain in the past.

A flurry of crowed swept about him, perching on tents and trees. Zoya was approaching, for they guarded her eternally. He saw the lights of her party exiting the forest below and making their way towards him. He went back into his tent to rest and await her. He couldn't feel for her the way he felt for Sonia. He could never love another so deeply. Zoya was familiarity. Zoya was purpose, as much purpose as could be found for him in this world. She was the queen and he was but her pawn, a reality that suited him perfectly. He had lost all desire for righteousness, for meaning. Those terms failed him long ago when he still cared, when he still opened himself to others. Zoya owned no part of his heart. He liked to believe he had no heart, but that was far from true. Sonia and Alla, they held his heart and always would. Betray him a thousandfold each, he would never give up his affection for them. They were unequaled in his lifetime. Nothing in his travels came close to the pleasure they had once given him and deep inside, he cherished this feeling. Without it, his heart might just fail its rhythm. Without it, the sun might never rise again. Without it, there was nothing.

Ilia dozed off as he awaited Zoya's approach. It was the quiet that woke him to find her kneeling before him, eyes downcast. Outside the tent he saw guards attentive and solemn. He stared at her for several minutes, unable to fathom what misfortune could justify her behavior. Finally, he raised himself from the cot and took her chin in his hand to bring her gaze even with his own. Her eyes were filled with tears that shed across her face in the flickering firelight. He lifted her into his lap and pressed her into his strong arms, breathing in the smell of her hair. "What is it that troubles you Zoya? There is nothing within Novgorod we have to fear."

She took his hand and wept into it, kissing it repeated him. "My lord, the news I bring you pains me to despair." She burst further into tears and fell to the ground weeping and kissing his bare feet. "Oh my love, how I wish you could spare you this pain."

He lifted her again, this time standing and holding her firmly before him. "Speak what you must say and have it over. Enough with this drama."

Her knees weakened and he firmed his grip to keep her standing. "They that defy your righteous reign. Those who detest your love. They have done you the gravest of harms my lord. Such an atrocity as my heart has not the strength to speak."

"Speak! Bear forth with it!"

Zoya turned her mournful face toward him. The darkness of her eyes looked as lakes of pure sorrow. "They burned her. Your sister, as a witch and staked her and her daughter on the road to the city." With this, she fell to the ground, his grip loosed, his mind a blaze of fury, his heart bursting within him. He let forth a moan of such despair he felt his life pouring out with it. No spear or blade could have pierced him deeper. He might as well have killed her with his own hands. That such a fate would befall someone so innocent, so good, so deserving of all the joys this desolate life had to offer. He fell to the dirt and remained inconsolable through the night and into the next day. For three days he rejected all who approached his tent including Zoya. His only command was that they bury her and the child with he dignity they deserved. He had not the strength to face her corpse for fear of the judgment he deserved of her.

On the forth night Zoya entered Ilia tent and lay against him, caressing his chest and kissing his neck. He pulled her against him and whispered he was ready.

That night the hilltop ran with blood as the seventeen of Novgorod's inhabitants were sacrificed in the turning of Ilia into a god. The conversion from innocent child to an undying demon was complete. Anything that had remained of Ilia was bled out upon those stones. Only Kazamir remained and his hunger was insatiable.

Sofia rushed through the gates of the monastery gripping the hands of her two children tightly and pulling them to run faster. Behind them the sky was darkened with whirling screeching flights of crows. Houses burned and madness lie around every corner. She felt the very belly of hell had swallowed her up. All she wanted was to protect her children. She rushed them further, pushing past the masses of weeping terrified souls towards the only voice of peace to be found. Archbishop Pimen was issuing a prayer and she sought proximity to him like he was the warmth of a fire. She pressed her two children into her dress and stood before Pimen and God, her humility absolute, her appeal for salvation unreserved.

She helped in preparation of food for the hundreds of people gathering for protection. Small parties of men would rush out into the streets to collect food and goods left behind in the houses of those who now sheltered here. They had to make it last. There was no telling when rescue might come, if ever. Prayer and fellowship were all they could rely upon.

Outside the gates hell darkened the landscape. Wolves and devilish dogs roamed the streets, searching for stragglers, potential converts and playthings for the ruthless savages drawn to Kazamir's inferno. The landscape blackened with desecration and impardonable viciousness. Had madness gone mad, this would be the face of it. Kazamir himself drew near the monastery, bore upon a golden litter burning on four corners with the heads of young virgins and carried by blinded priests, each castrated, their severed testes shoved within their mouths and sewn shut. They were led by Zoya, who chained the first two about the neck and rode before on a white stallion splattered red with the blood of the fallen. One of the priests began to convulse and vomit, the hot burn seeping through his nose to find exit. He collapsed to his hands and knees tearing at his lips as he suffocated on his gag. A spear was thrust through the back of his neck by one of Kazamir's henchmen as another priest was brought forward, his genitals severed and eyes gouged out. Zoya herself sewed the gonads within his mouth and the procession continued forward.

Dina finished the porridge her mother brought her, including the extra bread she'd given special to her only daughter. Her brother slept beside her in the dim light, the fire set far from them in the crowded courtyard. She pulled the ragged blanket about her and cuddled up against him for warmth and comfort. Her mother had yet to return, still caring for others, giving endlessly of herself as she always did. Dina felt something move against her and she flung the blanket off expecting a roach or a rat in this dreadful hall. But it was only her precious wooden reindeer, given to her when she was a babe. The horns had long been lost, yet she loved it so. She placed it on the floor of the hall and felt its smooth back.

Suddenly it moved. Her hand recoiled and she questioned if she was seeing things. The deer clearly began to walk across the floor, slowly but with terrifying certainty. She sat upright and pulled her blanket closer about her, unable to stop watching and lost as to what else to do. As it made its way steadily away from her, she saw yet another tiny figure on its way towards it. Identical in stature, she saw it for yet another carven deer. This figure had lost not only its horns, but tail and one of its back legs. The two met in the midst of the empty floor, nose to nose and both came to a full stop.

Minutes past in silence as Dina stared on the curious site, still unable to believe her eyes. She became aware of a boy creeping towards the toys, equally entranced by their magical behavior. As he drew near them, she began to panic and rushed out to grab her deer and pull back away from him. The boy fell back on his backside in surprise and let out a gasp. An aged laugh startled them both and the two children turned to see and old woman seated near them, her eyes closed in mirth, shaking in her joviality. She continued this for some time and then tossed a handful of crystal stones in front of her standing above them as if they provided her some curious insight. After several minutes of this, she spoke to the children. "Help me collect these my dears and gather your mothers as quick as can be. We have much to do in such little time."

Yaroslava was a witch that lived far from Novgorod, one of the few pagan souls left in all of Russia. She stood before the children and their mothers with a pride and love that was as welcome as it was a surprise. "You my young man are Pavel, son of Timor and your mother Alla, brother of Ilia." She turned to Dina, "and you my dear are sweet Dina, the only daughter of Ilia and his beloved Sonia." Silence held sway and the party looked upon each other with wonder. "My joy abounds to see you all together, fruit of my children and children's children. How I've loved you all from afar."

"You're my great-grandmother?" Ventured Dina.

"Yes my sweet. Estranged through religious differences with your grandfather."

"Where is my brother?" Burst Alla, desperate to hear word of him after all these years.

"He is no more. Ilia sold his soul to a darkness that has no name. Nothing remains of him but a walking corpse that hunts us as I speak, for it is your dear brother Alla who lost his way so desperately, so profoundly that the darkest of magic now falls upon us. He is the beast outside the gate. He is Kazamir the Destroyer."

"You spout lies! My brother has the heart of a saint!"

"The goodness your brother brought this world exist between us now." She gestured about them. "This group is the legacy of his kind and good heart, not

83

that monster that approaches. That beast is the failure of the modern world, not the fault of our sweet Ilia. But it is now up to use to harness this goodness and push back against the darkness. The love that Ilia brought to each of you is what will guide the safety of us all." She cupped her hands below her chin in a generous smile that lingered in the firelight.

The main gate was set ablaze by men who once swore allegiance to Novgorod and now set about its destruction. The forces defending the monastery fought back with all they had, but hope grew slimmer by the moment. The sky was dark with swirling screeching crows and packs of wild dogs ran about the outer wall, anxious for entry.

Yaroslava worked with the priests and silversmiths on sacred bindings to catch the demon and keep its forces at bay. Such knowledge had long been passed orally through the tradition, but without her, would be lost in the Christian era. Dina and Pavel helped by passing blessings across the five silver blades that would honor the lost soul of Ilia by binding the monster that paraded in his form.

Meanwhile the gate burned on. Turned men scaled the walls and pissed down from above on those sheltering in the monastery. The flocks of crows pressed closer, feeling the fall looming. Kazamir on his ghastly litter stood shouting for the gate to fall.

Rather than fall, the gates were suddenly opened to the wonderment of all. A small cadre of the most devout Christian souls with Father Fadey and Archbishop Pimen in their midst burst soundly forth, their path protected by a spinning silver jewel spewing holy water around them. They sang hymns with a strength and nobility in their voice. Their enemies fell back in confusion. The litter collapsed as the priests bearing it lay prostrate to the ground praising God for his mercy and power.

Zoya rushed forward and sliced open the guts of Father Fadey. He held on to her as he fell under her blade holding her down so the party could soldier on. Kazamir menaced before them, holding a burning head in each of his hands. They paid him no heed and circled the beast with their number singing praises to God with the might of their voices. From their number, Archbishop Pimen stepped forward and kissing the first of the silver blades, drove it about the heart of the monster continuing with the next and through the set of five until he lay succumbed and defeated before him.

Part VI
Gathering of
the gods

He rode his bike down the remaining stretch of of the Overseas Highway as the sun began its dramatic plunge into the sea. Seagulls spiraled and called above and the air felt alive and unchanging. And then his vision was captivated by but one thing. She stood embracing the wind, her arms outstretched to feel it between her open fingers. Her long dark hair wheeling behind her. Her sun dress flirting with her figure, hinting and demanding he imagine all that she had beneath it. He knew from that moment he belonged to her and she belonged to him.

They wed just two weeks later, they could not get enough of each other. Her name was Daphne. He was Basilio and ex-pat from Barcelona, having spent his college years in the States. They were two free spirits reaching each to other at a time when their futures were open and their hearts both longed for true romance, adventure and exploration. They honeymooned in Costa Rica, spurning any tour program and launching impulsively on their own. For that would be their shared life – risk, adventure, and romance. They agreed to settle for nothing less. They found a waterfall that sang as an orchestra into the crystalline pool at its base. They stripped each other playfully and leaped in. Exotic birds called from the trees around them and dragonflies buzzed quickly passed as they swam together to the other side near the falls. He took her in his arms and smothered her with his love for her. Her lips made his heart swell, the feelings she brought him could not be contained in his body and shone out with a brilliance of its own. She moaned slightly as he kissed her along her neck and then back across her face, gently fondling with his lips the tender mole she has beside her right eye. He loved that mole for it was hers and hers alone. Her blue eyes shone back at him and her gorgeous upright breasts glistened in the setting light. They made love among the rocks for hours. He worshipped her body, understanding it as no on had before. His fingers inside her made her quiver and she climaxed in powerful shudders again and again. He owned her completely. She never wanted freedom from his grasp. This moment could only last the rest of time. Time slipped by and they heeded not as the full moon blast across a cloudless sky. He lifted her in his arms and took her beneath the waterfall, where he ravaged her every way she could handle his manhood. Her cries of passion echoed amidst the splashing water and across the rock cave behind. She felt such total bliss she was unable to think and begged for him to stop, but he would not obey her, taking her from behind and spanking her wet ass, compelling her squeeze down on him and cum harder. She reached back to hold his balls, her eyes closed and rolling back in her head. She bit her lower lip and screamed out in the largest orgasm she ever felt, and the sound of this and the feel of her body tensing down on his cock was more than he could handle. She squeezed his balls harder and he flooded inside her in abundant waves of cum that left him aching from the emptiness of having surged all the pleasure and love he had deep inside her. He pulled her shaking form back up to him. Her knees were too weak to hold herself up. He grabbed her by her left breast and kissed her moistly across her face. She could do nothing but pant for breath, her eyes closed, a constant smile across her face. The only thought she could maintain was that this was pure happiness and she laughed quietly as he held her, reveling in his strong body, still erect, back inside her and still pumping the last drops of cum into her.

She sat amidst her euphoria on the wet black rocks beside the falling waters. Basilio had swum across to get their dry packs and bring back some food and drinks as she recovered herself before heading back to their campsite on the far side of the pool. She sat naked, his cum working its way out of her to the rock below her red ass, tender from his passionate harsh spanks. She wished she could keep all the warm slick wonder of it within her and squeezed in to try to pull it higher up, smiling to herself as she did so, loving the feel of it inside her. The moon played amidst the waves that splashed upon her feet. She was starting to get a bit cold, but didn't mind. She was too happy to care about any inconvenience. She saw his fine shape on its way back to swim across. He cock was still longer than normal, still thrilled as she was by the eternal love making they had experienced. He dove in with the dry bags and began to cross. She felt a prick on her thigh and turned to late to see the shape of a spider monkey creep silently away. She touched the spot and a drop of blood was on her finger. Her vision suddenly because blurred and her heart felt heavy. She gasped for breath and in a last second of panic wished to call out to Basilio before she slipped forward unconscious into the pool.

It was six months later that he was sitting at the side of the Overseas Highway, having just thrown his bicycle into the ocean. He could see the waves beating it back against the shore. He had a thermos she had given him for the honeymoon trip he'd now filled with Key Lime Martini from the Hog Breath bar and he held a glass he kept filling it to. It was the same drink they had together at that bar after leaving this spot where they had met. He was more drunk than he'd been in his life. He scratched at the five months of growth on his face and smelled the salty sea air. It still gave him the sense of timelessness, but it no longer felt alive. It was an unchanging, unemotional, unreactive timelessness. A cycle of unfeeling. A repeat with subtle changes, but the same outcomes. A sharp prick in his lower back caught his attention, though it took time for him to react to it in his state. He rubbed at the spot and continued to stare at the sea. His head felt hot suddenly and he rubbed his forehead.

"You're gonna burn here my friend, looks like you already have. Why don't you let me take you under some shade?" The voice came from a very tall dark-haired man with a monkey on his shoulder. Basilio found himself of two minds. He had come here to pass out drunk where he met Daphne, but he found the compulsion to follow this man to be irresistible. Adrik reached out his hand and helped Basilio to his feet, leading him to the Prius he had waiting for them at the side of the road. They went to the Green Parrot bar. Adrik ordered more of the Key Lime Martinis for both of them. Basilio was in too much of a daze to understand how he knew what to order. Perhaps he had told him at some point.

"I am Adrik by the way."

"Basilio." Is all he could answer, sucking in the next Martini, trying to clear the strange heat from his head.

"Basilio, Spanish?"

"Yes." Hoping the questioning would cease at that.

"Tell me about her."

The question struck him like a loaded tanker truck. He was flooded by all the images of their time together since they had first met, through their hasty marriage and their tragic honeymoon. Tears began to run down his face. Adrik placed his hand on Basilio's shoulder and looked him square in the eyes. The words began to flow out. The passion, the love, the desperation, the loss, the endless hospitals and doctors all giving the same answer. Nothing could be done, nothing could be found that caused it. She was there. Still alive, still beautiful. Still all his world. But she would not wake. His own sleeping beauty. He cried at her bed countless times. He shouted at her to revive! To return to him! He even slapped her once and shook her when no one was looking, tears streaming down his face, begging her to see him, feel him, understand how much he needed her to come back. He would slit his neck if that was what it took for her to wake and be herself again. Was it a bug bite? Was it genetic? What it something in the water? Was it stress? Had he overexerted her at the waterfall? Had she been coming down with something? He traveled the world for any doctor that could help. The wealth of his surname gave him nearly unlimited resources and he used them, but there was no improvement. No one could see a cause. No desperate measures provoked a reaction. She was his sleeping beauty, but his kisses did nothing for her. He could not find direction in his life outside of her care. It was all he wanted. Nothing else mattered. He ignored family and friends. He ignored every responsibility and he ignored his own health. He just wanted her to look him in the eyes again. He needed that smile once more. She was so close to him, but so far away.

These words streamed from him and he collapsed crying upon that table, knocking his drink over. Adrik ordered another and waited for Basilio to recover. The monkey placed a thorn into the glass and it sank to the bottom, a fog of dark mist flowing from it. Basilio sucked down the next glass and slammed it back to the table, again knocking it over. His head fell against the wood, his breath was troubled. He repeated her name at first with pain and agonized tears and slowly more as a mantra. Mephisto climbed upon his back and withdrew another thorn, stabbing him quickly behind the ear. Basilio batted at the it, thinking it an insect and Mephisto returned to Adrik to wait.

When Basilio lifted his head again, the words he spew, he knew not off. It was his passion, it was his feeling, but his short-term memory and his understanding had been taken from him. He spoke endlessly of her, describing every aspect of her personality, her laugh, her temper, her sensitivity, the fragility that made him want to protect her against the world. He went on and expounding her virtues to goddess level, his face formed as a carnival mask of pained sadness. Fixed, as if carved just for the purpose. The stream of tears running down his cheeks never having time to dry, always replenished.

"What if there were a way to bring her back Basilio?"

Basilio was in midst of clarification of her perfection and it took a minute for his mind to change perspective. "I would take anything. I would do anything. I would give anything."

"Good, you will have to do all three."

Over time Mephisto continued to drug Basilio and Adrik promised Daphne would return from her sleep and be with him again, if only he helped them on their mission. They travelled the world and in each place something extraordinary would happen. Something supernatural. Something that defied the senses of Basilio, but he had become a willing slave. He made no judgements and only thought his beloved. In Tikal, another cloudless night with a crescent moon above them, they went far from the national park, hacking deep into the woods where a single stone was buried beneath the deep entangling roots of a tree, vines and layers of growth and soil making it impossible to detect. Adrik and Basilio hacked their way through the growth and hit upon the stone. Hewing against it with axes it slowly broke away in fragments until an opening was revealed. They expanded this, stank stale air flowing out. Silently and dark as the night, a panther crept from this. As perfect and lithe as if it had never aged within this ancient stone crypt. Moments later came a man, dressed in 2500 year old Mayan dress. Buluc Chaptan stood before them. Adrik fell to his knees before the god as did Mephisto. Basilio collapsed back on ass, staring in disbelief. The panther sat beside him and he bowed himself before the ancient god.

They took the panther and Buluc Chaptan via Land Rover to the yacht Basilio had waiting for them on the coast. From there, they sailed to Venezuela where they chartered a helicopter to take them to the top of a tepui. The helicopter left, for a storm was approaching, and they fought through a heavy downpour to reach a bulging river that flooded over sheer cliffs to the valley below. Beside this river they worked again at the rock slowly breaking it apart in pieces until another opening was revealed. Widening this further a hand reached out and they released a second god, Mawarí, all three laying prostrate before him as the sky shook around them. The god leaped into the fast flowing stream and rushed over the side to fall the untold distance to the sliver of water that represented the river flow on the plain far below. Once the sky had cleared their helicopter took them back down and they drove their rented van to the place Mawarí awaited them.

Next they chartered a flight to the Mediterranean landing in Crete and chartering a boat to take them out to an area of vast open sea. They waited there until nightfall when the waters became rough and storms brewed above them. Through the churning waves rose a pinnacle of rock, encrusted with barnacles, crabs rushing off to return to the sea. Adrik and Basilio took a small raft and approached the rock, tying off to it and leaping upon the rock with their axes. They search about until Adrik chopped off some of the barnacles and coral and pointed to an area that looked to once have had a shape carved into it now worn by waves and time. They began to hack away at this as the waves crashed at their feet and once again an opening broke through. They worked this further and Adrik reached his hand within. For a time, there was no response, but then a hand did reach up. The oldest of the existing gods, Athanasius, was pulled back from his watery crypt.

It was under a half moon that they travelled through Cambodia to Angkor Wat, far off from the main temples amidst deep overgrowth they found an area of dark burnt rock. The lush vegetation left it as a stark dead outrage amidst the lavish greenery. They broke their way through this rock as they had time and time again. The stone was unforgiving, but they continued at it under the moonlight. Screeches in the night sounding the alarm of their peculiar activity. Finally, unlike the other stones, this black menace broke in two, the top slowly falling away heavily to the forest floor behind. They looked upon the gaping hole as the dust cleared and descried Narin, his arms upheld and they bowed before him.

The last two were in Russia, each protected under holy places that still held their sacredness. Adrik had prepared these two in advanced through bribery and they just had to wait for the mafia to do their job. They had paid a steep price to make sure nothing would go wrong, for the site of these would terrify even the strongest of men. Vasily and Kazamir would be waiting for them in an empty building in Saint Petersburg.

Six they had collected. The six that waited for the seventh to be created. Some had waited for thousands of years. The awakening of the seventh. The culmination of all that had been so far achieved. The dawn of the age of the gods.

Part VI
Two Doves for My Soul

He hit the downhill in full stride, his heart beating out a rhythm for the road. His focus was on his breath – in out in out, maintain the pace. A dark strewn shape lie across the sidewalk, as he drew closer it became the body of a black cat. He decided to turn his course and went down a side street. The world grew rapidly quieter, the din of the city consumed by the bright fresh foliage of the bushes and trees. He cut the next left hard at a pungent azalea and she was there. It was an instant and an eternity. The play of the sun on her long blonde hair as she leaned forward to plant the tulip in her hand. The graceful curves of her back under a delicate purple shirt above a spotted skirt. The elegance of her toes through her sandals. He fought to avoid crashing into her, over-stretching his step, missing the sidewalk, straining his right ankle with a strike of intense pain. He fell forward in his momentum bracing and rolling in a fall, grabbing his hurt leg.

She stood over him before he could recover his thoughts and his eyes met with hers. Grey and piercing they carried him away and he felt his heart race, the blood filled his ears and the sound of the world fell away. A stillness took the moment and stretched it into an unforgettable vista. The blue sky above her head, a small yellow butterfly that seemed to circle around the flowing hair that cascaded across her face as she reached to help him. She touched his ankle and he released his hold of it to feel the pair of her hands encircle it with a tenderness that overwhelmed the pain with the generosity of her care. He could see she was speaking to him, but the words were beyond him. He could not release himself from her eyes, they pulled him deep within and he felt himself diving into her soul never wishing to surface.

"We should get some ice on this. Can you try to stand and I'll help you into the house?" He felt the pull of her voice bring him back.

"Yeah, of course. I'm Jacob by the way, seems like I should introduce myself before you nurse me any further." Jacob smiled, gaining composure over his emotions.

She laughed, with a soft peaceful gentle sound that he knew he could never get enough of, "I'm Idalia, it's so nice to get the chance to trip you today."

Idalia supported Jacob as he pulled himself off the street and she took his right hand, holding him tightly across his chest with her left hand. Their first embrace, he thought. He would never find himself questioning how instantly he loved her, how she above all women was different. It didn't require thought or explanation, simply attention and devotion to something that was infinitely true and right.

When they reached the house a black cat followed them inside as Idalia aided Jacob to a chair. He smelled the luxury of her hair as she eased him back and he found himself closing his eyes to breath her deeply in.

"I'll be right back with some ice and a glass of water." She sailed off towards the kitchen and he could not keep his eyes off of her. If there was any pain in his ankle he wasn't even dimly aware of it. The universe had just pivoted and reset. There was a barren moonscape of daily life before and now there was a sunrise and he stood madly blinking in the blinding glare of Idalia.

"Do you always run like someones chasing you?" The laugh again, like music but also for his eyes to watch that face of hers light up.

"I'm training for a race in a three weeks. It's going to be competitive, but I think I can win." She handed him the water, still smiling and listening, her eyes examining him perhaps as deeply as he contemplated her. She pulled the ottoman in front of him and he lifted his leg upon it. She aided him in this and removed his shoe, taking the towel she'd filled with ice and wrapping it about the ankle.

"Thank you." Her smile went even wider and her eyes shone. Had he ever met anyone so naturally joyful? He felt a sensation in his chest start at this moment that would stay with him the rest of his days, as a place within him was made for Idalia. It would feel to him like she filled his chest almost completely with a soft ache that had only one salve – the thought, the presence, the very idea of Idalia.

The afternoon warmly passed on. She sat beside him with her own glass of water and they learned about each other's schools. They were both seventeen, she was three months younger than he was. That date now the second most important to him after the day he was experiencing with her now.

The conversation wound on naturally and pleasantly. They shared enthusiasm for the outdoors, athletics, eclectic music and campfires with friends deep into the night. She tossed her hair from her face and smiled across at him again. He wanted to pull her into his arms and never let go.

A branch scratched across the window and the darkening sky became apparent as a summer storm approached. "My mom can drive you home when she gets in, I don't have a car or I'd take you myself."

"I don't want to be a burden, I can call my dad to pick me up, he should be home by now." The thought of this afternoon coming to a close made his pulse quicken. If he could choose, it would last the rest of his life.

The doorbell rang and she went to answer it. His heart fluttered briefly from even the slightest pain of distance. A woman entered in her later twenties or early thirties. She had dark raven straight black hair and her eyes seemed to quickly analyze the situation.

"Hello, I'm Simone, I see you've had a run in with Idalia. Poor thing, she can be quite the man-killer." Idalia laughed and disputed this claim, insisting it was Jacob who was barreling unreservedly down the road. Jacob felt Simone restraining a reaction upon seeing him.

Jacob began to rise to his feet, but Simone stepped to him and pressed his shoulders back into the chair, leaning over to talking quietly near his ear. "Rest you, no need for formalities. How's this leg doing?" She removed the towel and pressed into the swelling, Jacob wrestled back the urge to wince as she eyed him closely. "Looks like you'll live. How far is your home from here, I'd be glad to give you a ride back when your ready." She placed the towel back and moved herself over to Idalia. "You left your gardening out which had me worried about you. Its about to pour."

Idalia laughed and thanked Simone for reminding her. "Excuse me Jacob, I'll be back in a minute. Hopefully I can beat this rain!" She rushed out the front door and he saw a beautiful blur swoop across the window to the place he first met her.

"Do you and Doll know each other Jacob?"

Jacob paused just slightly to incorporate the new nickname. "No, I just crashed into her today. We go to different schools, but are both seniors." Simone sat on the ottoman beside his leg and watched him carefully in silence for a moment. Her eyes suddenly flashed to the black cat sitting across from them, watching the entire afternoon from its position atop the couch. "And what are your thoughts Memphis? Whose to blame in this collision?" The sky suddenly opened in a driving downpour. Simone went to the window with a smirk as she watched Idalia clean up her unplanted tulips and tools. She headed down the hall and came back with another towel as the back door in the kitchen opened, Idalia entering soaked to the bone and filled with laughter.

"You'll have to excuse me Jacob while I get changed."

The downpour grew even more oppressive, thunder rolling angrily. "The sky is suddenly so dark." Simone spoke slowly as she approached the window, her right hand petting the cat. A wailing siren raced up the street and flashing red lights sailed past the house from an ambulance and soon after a firetruck and police cars.

"What's going on out there?" Idalia reemerged wearing jeans and a white top.

"Looks like an accident just up the road, grab me an umbrella please." Idalia went to the closet and handed an umbrella to Simone who headed out the front door to investigate. The dim flashing lights were still visible through the rain. Traffic was beginning to back up in front of the house. Simone stood within view on the sidewalk watching beneath the umbrella as the unanticipated finale to their afternoon unfolded.

The storm continued outside as they sat in the hospital waiting room. Idalia was devastated, her head in her lap and her long hair coursing amidst her arms folded tightly under her face. She was clearly forcing the world away from her and Jacob wasn't sure if he should try to console her or just give her space. Simone was again at the nurse's desk requesting an update. Jacob limped to the vending machine and purchased a bottle of water for Idalia, placing it gentle beside her. He so wanted to place his hand on her shoulder and say her mother would be fine, but the truth was his sense of dread was building.

He felt his heartbeat as the doctor came down the hall, each step foretold the answer. Idalia lifted her head and pulled her hair back to a mournful tear-stained look. His own eyes welled up, she doesn't wait for the doctor's words, her fragile form begins to quake in deep tragic sobbing. Simone swings around and folds her in her arms with a protective hug, burying Idalia's face and letting her release the full pain of her agony muffled against her breast. Jacob could only stand, his own tears running down his face for the loss of a woman he had never met.

He stared numbly out the window of the taxi taking him home. He couldn't even say goodbye to her. He felt so incapable as he watched her suffer. He felt the tug of distance as the car sped from the hospital. They hadn't had time to exchange numbers. He wished feverishly for something he could do for her, but there was nothing, nothing he could offer to replace such a loss she was feeling now.

He opened the door to the apartment, the television was on in the front room entertaining no one but Theo his shepherd. His father hadn't answered any of his phone calls, "Dad?" He went to his father's bedroom and pulled it open to see the man passed out across the bed, still wearing most of his work clothes. The last line of cocaine remained on the dinner plate beside him. Jacob pulled the door abruptly closed and went to his own room.

Memphis, a hot August night in a worn out apartment on day 14 of a massive drug and alcohol binge. Someone was laying partially across him on a cramped bed. The radio continued to blast loudly but muffled from somewhere in the room. He moved the girl from him and sat up with his feet off the bed. He felt another body and saw two men sleeping on the floor. These were the moments when he questioned things, when his frustration and hopelessness were at the lowest ebb and he could recall back six months to when his marriage to Rebekah was his life's meaning and his career was still intact. Such thoughts were fleeting as the manic hum of the chaos that overtook them would return.

He went into the bathroom and filled a Bud Light can with water from the sink drinking it down a sore dry throat as he contemplated himself. This was no longer working. Memphis was not keeping his mind off of it – the vibrating anger, dipped in a black-tar soul-wrenching sorrow was returning. He rubbed at his eyes which were already tearing up and felt the pain in his head of fuck this world and everyone in it! If he stayed here any longer it would be another Boston and that was not going to happen. He'd continue his way to Austin if he could make it that far. He found his shirt and pulled his pants from under the lion tattooed man on the floor. The tattoo reminded him of something the man had said to him last night – or the night before. The most intense trip he'd experienced was in small town Georgia. He'd been temporarily institutionalized at a psych hospital. The dealer promised him he'd see and feel things he would have no words for and these sensations would be life-changing. What he actually experienced was nearly fatal to him and he could remember nothing from the four days following the trip besides a nonstop blur of violent and maddening imagery. Angry dogs, massive sexual orgies, lions, blasts of indescribable colors shooting into his eyes, and people after people being murdered.

He turned the man over and shook to wake him up. "Hey, hey, dude, wake up. Come on, get up."

"What? Fuck man."

"Tell me where in Georgia you had your bad trip?"

"Say what?"

"In Georgia, where were you institutionalized?"

"Uhhh, Milledgeville. I got out last fall."

"That's where you had that trip?"

"Yeah, off Usery Street, south of town. I stayed there for a few weeks, but that stuff almost put me back in Central State. I had to get out of there."

"Usery Street? Got a name?"

"Ask for Tyco, he has access to everything including the crazy shit they gave me." He left him alone and found his shoes.

"You should just stay here man, you don't want to mess with that shit I'm serious." He didn't give the room or the town another glance as he headed out the door and back to the road.

That guy didn't fucking understand. They didn't understand. No one could understand why none of it, just none of it mattered. It was all complete bullshit and no one else had the balls to admit it.

"Breath. Breath. Breath" He repeated mentally, repositioning his weight in the blocks. A timeless moment awaiting the signal to start, his mind pushing for no other thoughts, yet fleeting images of a thousand ideas would suddenly zoom past until he again pushed them away and steadied his mind on the track. Just the track, the color, the texture, how the impact of his step felt as it pressed and forced the maximum he could receive from the tarmac. Breath, keep breathing. His mind was at ease, his focus secured, the race had already begun and he was pulling forward with the leaders. He heard nothing, felt nothing but the soles of his feet and the beat of his heart. Push harder, you have more. He felt a cleaner more efficient stride than he had ever felt before. His heart soared as he knew he was unbeatable at this stage, there were no other racers. The finish approached, he pressed towards it, the adrenal pumping a magical anticipation bigger than he could have anticipated as he crossed the line, a feeling of absolute bliss.

The loudspeaker called out his name, "Jacob Skyler of Lakeside with a time of 20.59 in first place." He heard his classmates cheering and screaming. Someone handed him a water bottle and he pulled it down as the crowd gathered in and the award ceremony begun. From the podium's height a flash of bright on the far left of the crowd drew his attention. It disappeared in the bustle but his eyes remained lock until she came briefly back in view. The blood pounding in his ears twice what it had during the race, he bolted from the podium and plowed towards her, leaving the presentation in disarray. She was laughing as he reached her and he simply sucked her tightly into his arms and held her. They embraced each other silently, neither having need to speak or wanting the moment to pass. She smelled so good in his arms, more vividly than he could have imagined. He held her tighter and she laughed again and moved her hand gently from his back to his shoulder. His coach came up from behind, "Jacob, there's time for this later, let's get back to the medal ceremony."

"How did you know?" He pulled back not fully letting go of her to look into her eyes.

"You said you had a race in a few weeks."

"Jacob, come on!" He let go over her, holding her right hand as long as he could before releasing it and going back to the ceremony. He kept his eyes on her the entire time and she became shy from the attention as the crowd looked to her. They walked off together as soon as the opportunity came and took a grassy path outside the track field.

"I came by your house several times but no one was there."

"I know, I'm staying with Simone. She's my Godmother. I can give you my address." She looked at him to see that he wanted this.

"I'd love that." He reassured. "I wrote you letters, didn't you get them?"

She looked down as she answered him, "I know. I just ... needed some time for myself. I'm sorry."

"Don't be, I understand."

She looked up at him, her eyes rimmed in growing tears, "No, I should have let you know —" The world began to spin as he fell into the softness of her eyes, he pulled her to him and they sank into a deep kiss. He held her face gently between his hands, every moment of happiness and elation being eclipsed in this eternal instance of absolute bliss.

"I've missed you so much." He breathed into her hair clutching her to him desperately. She nestled her head against his shoulder and chest wrapping her arms tightly about him. "I missed you too." He pulled her in front of him again and kissed her once more, then upon the cheek and with her face again in the care of his hands he ever so gently and tenderly kissed her left eyelid, feeling the warmth on his lips.

They gazed in each other's eyes, holding hands and feeling their way across each other's palms and fingers, wanting to know everything, feel everything.

"I started running." She said, with a content smile below adoring eyes that told of her complete satisfaction in the splendor of the experience. "I kept hoping I would find you out there, maybe run into you again." They both laughed and kissed again, this time even deeper and more hungrily. They walked for hours in the park behind the field. She ran to cope with the loss of her mom, driving herself harder each day to push back at the pain. He showed her the proper way to stretch before and after a run. She showed him the shoes she'd purchased and he was both moved and impressed. His heart was sailing a million miles above the Earth. Everything felt almost too real, so devastatingly perfect.

The sun coursed across the sky as they learned the joy of being together, building an intimacy that held back nothing. Everything was exposed between them, no secret places too tender to open. He walked her home, never letting go of her hand. Her laughter always came easily and he rejoiced in its softness, tugging her near when this became unbearable and meeting her half way to another kiss. They reached Simone's house, a pair of crows landed in a nearby pine tree. He could see Memphis looking out the window of the living room.

"Come in and stay with me a while." She looked warmly up at him.

"How can I say no to those eyes?" They shared a final long kiss and went inside.

Usery Street 9:15pm. He was walking it for the third time trying to find anyone who knew Tyco. Either they were not saying or he wasn't there. The door to the shack of a house he was passing on his left flew open and two young men burst out and ran for him. He backed up and the first one swung, just missing as he leaned away while the second man punched him in the kidney and he fell to his knees.

"What the fuck you want?"

"I heard I could score here." He held up his hand, holding himself steady with the other. "I'm just looking to score man."

"Who told you to come here?"

"This guy in Memphis. He told me to ask for Tyco."

"What the fuck guy told you that?"

"I think… I think his name was Reggie. He shaved his head and had a lion on his back."

The answer was unsatisfactory and the blow to the back of his head threw sound out and iron into his mouth. The remaining kicks to his ribs were dimly recognized as everything spun out.

He came to again from the flies crawling into his mouth. He was laying in the bare red clay, the smell of dried dog shit surrounded him. Everything hurt, especially the lump on his head and the pain in his ribs. He tried to sit up and felt a chain choking into his neck. He was chained to a spike for the dog. His shoes were missing and his socks. He felt unbearably thirsty. He worked at the chain around his neck to free himself. A little girl was standing ten feet in front of him watching and when he looked up at her she ran off around a garage. He felt it better to leave the chain on than try to free himself and risk another beating. He could hear a screen door open and her small voice making others aware of his revival.

This time there were three of them, two he recognized from earlier, the third was a thin young black man with a neatly trimmed goatee dyed white. He wore an expensive black Sean Jean outfit and bright red sneakers. His eyes stayed behind designer sunglasses and he squatted down in front of him to show a fearlessness and full display of his jewelry.

"Why you looking for me?"

"I'm just looking to score —"

"Why you come to fuckin Milledgeville to score? Who the hell goes from Memphis to Milledgeville?"

"Because Memphis didn't have what I need."

Tyco thought about this for a while. "What's your name?"

"Pascal"

"Okay Pascal, what is it you think I can give you that you need?"

"Escape." Pascal rubbed at his aching ribs. "Something that changes everything. Something that makes me feel again."

"You want to feel? You didn't feel Donovan kicking you in the head last night?" Tyco laughed at himself as did Donovan and the third man. Tyco appeared to be less agitated with the answers Pascal was giving. "What is it you want to feel?"

"I want to feel different. I want my world to change."

"Brother sounds like what you need is a preacher." Tyco stands up with this, "Change my world. Change my world. I can change your world mutherfucker if that is what you are looking for." With this he drew a Glock from his pocket and pressed it up against Pascal's face below his left eye. "Is this what you want, huh?"

Pascal didn't respond and continued to look Tyco in the eye. Tyco withdrew the weapon and walked away. "Get him some water."

It was drawing towards evening before Tyco returned again with his two companions. He brought Pascal a hot dog, cold just out of the refrigerator. Pascal swallowed it in a few greedy bites and drank more from his water.

"Mr Memphis. Change my world. Shit. How you gonna pay for that huh? You didn't have but $36 in your wallet."

"I have more in my car."

"Yeah? Where's it at?"

"I parked it over by Grits and walked here. It's a red M3 with about $600 in the glove box inside of the owner's manual."

Tyco looked at him for a while silently and then the three of them walked away. About fifteen minutes later he heard a car start up and leave down the road towards Grits. Another twenty minutes and it returned followed by his M3. The discussions he could hear from around the corner of the garage were livelier and with more laughter. Donovan and his friend came around the barn and picked him up to his feet, unlocking the chain from his neck and leading him into the garage. It was musty and dark as they placed him on an old stained couch patterned in rat droppings, dried insects bodies and spider webs. They moved a brake assembly to give him more room. Tyco came in with some Michelob and tossed one to Pascal. He pulled a chair over by the couch and lit a cigarette for himself. "Memphis man." He said laughing with a wide bright smile as the smoke streamed from his mouth and nostrils. Pascal opened the beer and breathed it in, hoping to dull the throb in his head. Tyco, Donovan and the third man laughed at this, "Alright then alright. You're okay. So you come to me for a serious trip, something that can really fuck you up?"

"That's what I've been fuckin trying to tell you."

"Why you think I have something so special you come all the way here to me for it?"

"I've been going anywhere I hear might have what I need. Chicago, Detroit, Boston, Memphis, if I don't find it here I'll look for it in Austin and keep going to Mexico from there."

"Is that right?"

"That's right."

"Chicago, Detroit, Boston, Austin – Milledgeville got to represent!" Tyco rose from his chair. "I tell you what. For $600 I'll give you your trip, but you may not like what you get. That ain't my problem."

"Donovan, get Memphis man something to eat." Tyco turned to Pascal once more. "Tomorrow I'll have your fix for you." He grew a wide smile again, "You ain't gonna make it to Austin I assure you that, but you may not like what you get."

Jacob pulled up to the church parking lot in his aged Integra and stepped out with a broad smile across his face. "Hey Elias." He called to the weathered black man pulling on a cigarette sitting in the shade of the church wall.

"Hey there Jacob, how you doing today?"

He walked up to Elias and shook his hand. "Very well, yourself?"

"I'm doing fine, I'm doing fine. You got that thing running again eh?"

"Yeah, I had to replace the water pump this time. I'm hoping that's the end of it or I'll need to ask for more hours."

"I hear ya."

"Have you seen Idalia?"

"Course, she back in the garden as usual."

"Cool, see ya later!"

"Stay cool man."

"You too."

Jacob rounded the back of the church and saw Idalia bent down amidst the squash. The entire back lot of the church had been turned into a garden and her dedication to it humbled him.

"Hey you."

She turned to face him, her golden hair tucked away beneath a straw panama she'd decorated herself. "Hey Jacob! Ready to kill some bugs? These squash beetles are making me just want to pull this all out and start over."

"No need for something so rash when you've got your own private bug reaper."

"You might change your mind when you see this invasion. They're just everywhere."

He took her hand and smiled at her. "I can't think of a better challenge for my afternoon than killing bugs for you." He dipped below the rim of her hat and gave her three of the gentlest of kisses each with a slow pause in between as if there was all the time in the world for them to share.

The church was owned by the organization that Simone worked for Walking Together which provided education programs for recovering drug addicts and the homeless who chose to attend. It was Idalia's idea to use the back lot of the church for a garden to feed them as well. There were no church services there, though he often saw the pews upstairs being used for prayer. The classes and community always happened downstairs in the large gathering room.

He heard Idalia's gentle laughter above him and looked up to see her smiling face under the shadow of her hat. Her gloved hands were on her hips and she looked for all he could bear as someone he needed to throw over his shoulder and tickle. "Your hands are so yellow from squashed squash beetles." She laughed.

"Its quite stylish I hear, better than a manicure and far cheaper."

"Yes, bug mire is a fantastic hand softener."

"Aren't you two looking all domestic!" Simone came into the garden from the church. "My two garden dreamers."

"Hey Simone." Idalia smiled to her. "How's everything looking for tonight's classes?"

"Wonderfully. If we have the kitchen open with your help, we shall likely have a full house."

"As long as they love squash!" That playful laugh again, "I planted far too much squash I'm afraid. But we'll also have egg plant, the last of the spinach and quite a bit of beans. Oh, and the first of the garlic!"

"Sounds delicious, I'm looking forward to it. Jacob, are you helping with the meal preparation?"

"He's in charge!" Idalia piped in before he could respond. It was true, he had decided to give a try at the meal tonight. He'd been helping Idalia with the previous meals here and when they cooked together at Simone's house. He was also cooking more at home.

Simone laughed at them both and headed back towards the church, "I don't know what I am going to do with you two."

The couch was a marked improvement from the dog run and Pascal eased his aches with a case of cheap beer and junk food. He slept off as much as he could and woke towards the next evening to a party in the yard. A stereo was blasting Akon. He sat up and rubbed the back of his head, grabbing another beer from the floor and noticed the cigarette smoke. Tyco was seated off to the side watching him and started to laugh. "Mr Memphis. How are we feeling today, hmmm?"

"Right as rain."

"Right as rain. Right as rain." Tyco took another drag, "Well... let me see what I can do about that for you."

Pascal perked up at this. "We finally getting started?"

"Yeah, we startin something. Let me tell you, where it takes you, how long you'll be there, is up to you. You stay in here until its over, then you get the fuck out. I don't want to see you again." He picked up a glass of a dark liquid beside his chair and handed it to Pascal.

Tyco got up and headed slowly to the door. "No refunds, you'll get what you deserve."

The drink smelled of fresh blood, licorice, and something else that made him gag before even trying it. Pascal lifted it to his lips and dipped it back for a gulp. It was appalling and he fought to keep from heaving it back up immediately. "Best to drink it fast and get it over with." Tyco suggested with a laugh, still lingering at the door to see if Pascal would finish it. Holding his breath, Pascal gulped it down with force, swallow after swallow he fought back the urge to expel it until the glass was drained and he moaned and leaned forward with his head between his knees.

The door opened and Tyco stepped out to join the party. Pascal grabbed his beer to drown the taste in his mouth and then sprawled back across the couch.

After an hour with nothing he feared this entire endeavor was a bust. This was supposed to be it! The trip of a lifetime, mind altering, life-ending if it had to be. But there was absolutely nothing. Pascal dug into the coin slot of his jean's front pocket and pulled out his last Mad Hatter, removing it from its rice paper and laying it on his tongue. Austin was now on his mind. The whole East coast and Midwest little more than an expensive pony ride. There had to be a reality out there he could knock heads with. Something that would actually fight back when you punch it.

It did not seem that long before the LSD kicked in. There was no noise, his ears did not seem to be registering anything. The roof above him was only one of a series of realities that kept changing as he stared up – night sky, day sky, storm sky, trees moving, shrinking, growing -- everything in flux. He lifted himself up and found everywhere he looked this was repeating, the garage and house disappear and trees grow up and grow down, birds rushing and the occasional rabbit or possum. He thought about standing and walking out, but that thought was jarred by the sudden cacophony of sounds, voices, pleading, screaming he felt himself funneling and his vision became dark with nothing but sparks of dim yellow and red as the volume in his head changed from voices and sounds to a dim thrumming that vibrated and pulled him along a preset path. He could not tell when things were happening, the order of events was lost upon him. Time was bound so tightly the result of an occurrence happened before itself. This drew out further until he could not tell before or after from now, they lost all meaning and became simply awareness. Awareness removed all anxiety as there was no anticipation, everything was eventual. Distance became insubstantial as space folded to a singularity of experience, the events of life a capsule he held in his hand. In holding the capsule he was aware of the touch of it, the weight it bore down on his palm, pushing through and into him, his heart pounding madly as the entire universe coursed through as his blood. He felt the touch of everything at once. Life, birth and death. Countless death. Murderous, brutal and heartless.

The vortex of his mind sped further and at a relentless pace. He felt the frenzy would simply tear him apart, yet caring neither if it did or did not. A new sensation developed and he arched physically on the couch upon receiving it. The swirl of motion forked into a second much smaller vortex. He was aware of it, but could not comprehend it. Did this represent an alternative pathway for his life? Could he peer within two separate futures and choose the course to take knowing full well the trajectory of each, the joys the sorrows he would face? He could not feel within the second stream, it was opaque and unaware of him. Yet it grew in significance. Another potential came to him that this represented his conclusion and perhaps it was approaching. Perhaps he would not survive this journey and this was the black hole for his soul extending itself to encompass him thoroughly. He bent from it, finding somewhere deep within him the will to survive. As fleeting and weak as it was, it had an existence. The second vortex grew larger until it equalled or surpassed the first in size. The two tumultuous spirals sang wildly through his mind, he began to feel them through his fingers and toes and soon everything felt of a hot brilliant fire. He was certain he had stopped breathing and told his heart to simply pause for the moment. The two spirals fragmented simultaneously into a hundred million separations intermixing, reconnecting, splitting further and again rejoining endlessly and feverishly. Nothing was the same for the briefest moment, all is flux, all is chaos. He felt the spirals as strings of a harp and his soul walking over these sounding off notes that each spun in their own direction for him to travel up, down, under, behind, before, or never. The sound grew higher and the brightness increased. He felt it electrically through his body in violent painful spasms one after another. Sensation became sharper and more delicate and vision was fading to a consistency of white snow, muffling out all sound, freezing out all feeling until there was nothing but silent empty white.

His eyes fell open to the darkness of the garage. He was aware of the calmness of his own breath. He now saw more than a single lifetime, held the knowledge of generations, felt the agony of another's suffering from mistakes that so dimunized his own to press them into nonexistence. His life had a sudden and compelling meaning, the confidence of its purpose pulsed hungrily in his ears.

k

Jacob finished stacking the dishes and went back to check on Idalia. She was still curled up asleep across three chairs, her panama hat covering her head from the overhead lights. He watched her a moment, her body rising and falling slightly with each breath. Her delicate feet, tanned from hours in the sun and striped from her sandals.

He could hear Simone and Elias cleaning up the room following the class as the last of the students left. He helped them arrange the chairs and stack the paper and pencils back in their baskets.

"You did a wonderful job with the meal Jacob. I can't thank you enough for the effort you're putting in here for us."

"It's no problem."

"No problem? Maybe not, but it means a great deal to me and to Idalia too. Your help's making a real difference in people's lives."

"I'm just doing what I can Simone. You're the one who is turning people's lives around. I couldn't begin to –" He trailed off, getting emotional as he thought of his father's drug problems.

"Jacob? What's wrong? Something bothering you?"

He thought of telling her. How she might turn it all around, get his dad out of this madness. He would go months without lapsing and then suddenly, it was back. Ever since mom died, he'd never been the same. He'd never been able to regain himself from the loss of her. Instead, he went inward to a world of drugs and escape. Jacob could feel it as he touched the doorknob of the apartment. Last night, he didn't finish turning the key to unlock the door. He felt what he was going to find behind that door. He felt the anger and frustration of it building inside his throat and he just turned back and ran. He ran most of the night and slept the rest in the back seat of his car.

"No," He focused back on Simone. "Sorry, I just didn't sleep well last night. Getting kind of tired."

"Okay, well why don't you wake up Idalia. Its time for us to lock up and head out of here."

He went back to where Idalia lay and kneeled before her closely. He blew gently on her bare shoulder. She didn't react. He leaned closer and blew again across her neck. She jumped up and threw her arms around him laughing with delight at surprising him.

"You were awake?"

"I was watching you through the holes in my hat." She admitted. "You're quite the handsome devil you know."

"Is that what you think?"

"It is."

"Lucky me then."

"I'd say so."

He picked her up into his arms and spun her around quickly. She held her hat in an outstretched arm singing "Weeee" as her hair swirled up. He pulled her back up closely in his arms and placed his lips on her forehead closing his eyes. When he was with her, there was no elsewhere, no other, yet to come or has been.

Only us and now.

The drink Tyco had made Pascal had been found written by his father in a drawer after the old man got killed in a car wreck. There were several other recipes as well, but when he'd tried some of these, the results had been quite devastating on his customers, many of who were still in Central State as a result of the episodes. This one was unpredictable as well, but if your mind was strong enough, it took you to places nothing else would. Tyco himself wasn't interested. He wasn't interested in much concerning his old man. They had never had a clear understanding between them. He was always pushing him as a kid towards something bigger that he claimed he was a part of, but would never explain in detail. Whatever that thing was, it died in that car wreck.

Pascal stood outside the plantation front gate. The gate had actually fallen away from disrepair following a major storm and there was now simply an iron chain blocking the way with a Private Property sign attached to it. Other signs warned of No Trespassing and there was a large For Sale sign as well. He closed the door on his Chevy truck and climbed over the chain and walked down the overgrown roadway leading to the mansion. Everything vibrated with history. Things had changed, there were modernizations, but the plantation was still what it always had been. He walked past the mansion, badly in need of painting, but otherwise in stable condition. It had been occupied until the last few years so hadn't had enough time to fall into complete disrepair. The two Pied Crows led him on. They had begun following him once he stopped by the cemetery to view the mausoleum of Aquilla, where they sat perched as guardians. Now they led the way past the barns along the stream and back through the woods, beyond the woodshed until they led him beyond the property to the cave where Clarissa had convalesced so many years before. They perched themselves atop this cave and he looked inside waiting. After a few minutes a first and then another sets of eyes peered out from the darkness releasing their characteristic maniac laughter. Pascal laughed back in return. The game was about to start.

Pascal opened the door to his apartment and Tyco enters with a firm gait through the hall and into the living room with a dramatic view above Peachtree Street. The night was vibrant and charged. He heard Pascal seating himself in the couch behind him.

"There's going to be some serious feedback soon, you know that right?"

"You don't think we're ready for that?"

"It's coming soon, I guess we find out." Tyco turned to face Pascal. "Why you want it to play out like this? I'd feel better with a lower profile."

"There is no other profile. It comes to this no matter what we do. We only have control over the timing. Timing is now."

"Okay Sun Tzu. Shit, you was a ballsy motherfucker two years ago when you walk in on me in Milledgeville, but whoever the fuck you are now? I just hope to fuck you know what you're getting us into here. These motherfuckers will eat you alive. They don't care about all this money you got and your freaky ass laughing dogs, they will rip you open and eat your heart, you know what I'm saying?" Tyco paced as he spoke, a change from his normal composure of the past two years.

"They'll hit us." Pascal paused until Tyco felt that was all he was getting back. Finally Pascal concluded, "Then we'll know what they have to hit us with."

The afternoon sun was relentless, but Jacob was unaware of it. He felt nothing other than euphoria as he ran down the city blocks. She made everything more amazing. The play of light in the windows of the houses he past, the singing of the leaves as a breeze blew through them, even the sound of the traffic was a pleasure to his ears with a harmony that said she is close and she hears the same soundscape you do. They shared this world experience together and nothing could be more worthwhile.

He crested the hill and far below she was there, running ahead of him. He beamed, his whole chest lighting up with a delicate ache of need. He charged faster, clearing the distance between them. She either heard of sensed his approach and looked behind smiling and speeding up to race him. He laughed and chased down the remaining distance and she slowed for him to snatch her into his arms and swing her about in a circle, kissing her hot sweaty face repeated with his. They laughed together in a hot embrace, luxuriating in the sensuality of it.

"I've thought of nothing but you since yesterday."

"How did you get any sleep then."

"What makes you think I did?"

"In that case I should be able to beat you today."

"You'll never have a better chance." They laughed and held on to each other. He tasted the salt from her neck and nibbled her earlobe until she squealed from it.

They ran together. They ran to the church of Walking Together. Idalia ducked around the side of it to hide from him. He chased after her and she raced around the back laughing. As he turned the corner after her, he had to pull short for she had stopped and was watching a mockingbird in the grass. It looked to be injured and she watched as it worked to catch its breath and stared back at them. A pair of crows landed on the roof of the church behind them.

"I think its wing is hurt" He approached her slowly not to scare the small bird. The bird tried to fly away from his approach, flailing and unwieldily landing back in the grass between the garden rows.

"We have to get him help." She insisted, following after the bird who continued to try to fly away through the garden to the old unmanaged hedge behind it. The bird hopped and flailed under the hedge through a small opening at the base of the bush. Idalia looked back at him with a smile. "We can't give up now." She laughed and crawled under the opening. Jacob followed immediately after her.

"Isn't this incredible!" She was laughing and looking at him with wide eyes. They were in a quiet secluded clearing past the hedging with mature fir trees on all sides. It was silent and intimate, wild rosebushes dotted the area and the grass was high and lush green. "I didn't know we had all this, is it still part of the church property you think? I can't find the little bird though." They searched for the wounded bird in the little clearing, but it was nowhere to be found.

Meeting in the middle she looked at him with laughter in her eyes. He poked her nose and lifted her into his arms. She wrapped her arms about his neck and pulled in for a kiss. "I love you, you know." The words vibrated through him. He felt it had been true, but to actually hear the words he felt his face go red. He kissed her passionately, "I've loved you from the day I was born Idalia, its just been my journey to find you." She smiled and kissed him again.

"So this is forever?"

"Forever and again." Their faces touched and they gently felt each other's contours, delicately kissing the other's features repeating "I love you" with the softest of whispers.

Damien felt the smell of the wheels turning on the El Dorado as it pulled up to the abandoned house. It was just another smell, or was it a color in the orchestra that pounded inside him as he lay sprawled across what was once a kitchen floor with his back leaning in where the refrigerator stood long ago. Time flicked and bumped erratically for him. Ecstatic bodies pulsating and shaking, the dog in his face, a crow stabbed through his heart, the sound of the footsteps approaching the house, the kick of the boots. Who?

Damien smiled, "Thank you." The room grew darker and heavier. The approach of the boots down the hall. Who? The face of the Great Dane, its breath like that of something long dead, wetly entering his nose. The El Dorado. Who? The back of a hand covered in rings. "Thank you." He repeated. The El Dorado. The euphoria of power to control others. The street. Who?

Delarius pulled the El Dorado to the side of the road and exited, opening the rear passenger door and the two Great Danes exited. He reached in and pulled Damien from the trunk, dragging the small young man by the arm and shoving him into the rubble and weeds of the abandoned lot. Grabbing Damien's left hand he places it on the rocky ground and lifts a rock above his head. "I'm giving you one last chance Damien. You better clean up right fuckin now and tell me who you've been buying from."

Damien's eyes rolled in his head, only making out sounds and the occasional word. Visions of ritual sacrifice and arching aching bodies filled with need. Then the spike of pain, what was that?

Delarius tossed the rock away letting go of Damien's arm and again hefted Damien from the ground and to his feet giving him three fast strikes to the face. "A name Damien, give me a name!"

Damien saw only flashes of lights, the sensation of rain, a flock of birds surrounding him, a ringing phone, Delarius, stones. The order meant nothing. There was no order, everything was jetsam in a fast flowing river.

Delarius throws Damien down as the rains began to build and headed back to the car with the dogs. He answered the voice on the phone, "Yeah, alright good. I'm there in five. That fucker so much as move you cut his sack. We clear?"

Pascal parked the M3 in the church parking lot and climbed out into the heavy rain, placing the backpack on and throwing the heavy industrial garbage back over his shoulder. It was 2am and raining as he rested the bag behind the rear door to the church basement removing one of the immobilized crows from within it. He pulled out a chain of keys and began trying them each in turn until he hit the one that worked. Once inside he lit the flashlight and pulled the throw rug from the center of the room revealing a large flat stone surface in the midst of the tiling. He placed the flashlight on the ground casting light across the stone and laid the bird on the midst of it. Removing his pack he took out a canister and undid its lid setting it beside the stone. He then removed a black cloth and unfolded it to reveal a set of metal blades, each ending in five sharp prongs. He dipped this within the canister and then drove it into the crow sinking it into the stone with a noticeable reverberation. The bird began to struggle, weakly from the narcotic used to drug it earlier.

Picking up the canister and second blade, he dowsed the flashlight and left through the door grabbing the bag. Walking through the garden, he crawled under a gap in the soaking hedge and into the clearing behind. Dropping the bag in the tall drenched grass he pressed some of it down and felt across the ground with his hand, then returned with one of the birds placing it on the spot he had chosen and dipped the blade into the canister and finally piercing it through the heart of the crow. It struggled briefly and then went limp. He withdrew the blade and repeated this again and again across seventeen birds until his bag was exhausted. As he slew the birds the grass below let forth a pale blue glow.

He placed the carcasses back within his bag and used the cloth to mat up the blood and innards that had shed during the procedure, checking with his flashlight to be sure and lifting the grasses back as best he could, covering as much of his tracks as possible, he made his way back through the cemetery. Placing the bag and backpack in the trunk of his car he went back into the basement of the church. The air was static and the stone no longer looking to be stone, emitted a green pale light. The crow still struggle under the blade that pierced it. He withdrew the blade and freed the bird, which stood back on its own. He cleaned the area where it had lain on the stone and placed the carpet back down across it, lifting the bird and bringing it with him out the door where he cast it to the sky where it flew off through the shower of droplets into the dark. He locked the door behind him and, starting the M3, left down the road.

Idalia stared at the figure sprawled amidst her beans in the garden behind the church. His left hand was clearly broken. His feet bore wounds from stumbling across rocks and broken glass without shoes. She rushed to the church to get Simone.

"Simone, there's someone unconscious in the garden. They need to get to a hospital."

"Elias, can you help us please?"

"I sure can." Elias lifted Damien from between the bean poles and carried him back to the church basement. They laid him on the carpet and Idalia got some warm water in a bowl and some rags. Simone dialed 911.

Damien's eyes slowly opened, drawn by the gentle touch of Idalia washing his wounds. She smiled pleasantly at him as he looked uncertainly upon her. "Hey there, you okay?" She asked.

Simone continued to provide emergency with the location and details. "He's about 15 years of age – hold on looks like he's conscious." She leaned down over him. "Hi there, can you tell me what your name is?"

Damien looked on, a feeling of confusion growing. The high had long worn off and he was mired within a dense fog of uncertainty, anxiety and a deeper impending sense of terror. He wanted to run and his heartbeat started to increase.

"He's not responding and he doesn't have any identity on him." Simone walked away and continued to speak with emergency services and Idalia came back to continue to wash his wounds. "If the water is too warm let me know." He looked back at her and felt her touch through the cloth. Her hair kept spilling across her face and down her neck. "Are – are you a miracle?" He asked, Idalia paused, startled by his sudden voice and the peculiar question. Simone repeated her questioning, but that was the only words Damien spoke that day.

Elias helped him up to sit in a chair and wait for the ambulance to arrive and Idalia wrapped a blanket around him. He watched as she moved around the room, talking to Simone and preparing the room for the upcoming classes that afternoon. He watched her as she would glance occasionally at him, he watched as she placed the books and pencils and papers around the tables. She calmed him to a level he never experienced before. All the terrors, all the madness, all the anger was gone.

The EMTs from the ambulance knocked on the door to the church. Simone came over to explain things to Damien. "Okay, we're gonna get you to the hospital and make sure you're okay. I don't want you to worry, everything is going to be fine, okay?"

The EMTs helped Damien onto the gurney and out to the ambulance, his eyes locked on Idalia until she was out of site.

Marcus exited the Pink Store, a crow staring at him from atop the streetlight, and got back into his Celica heading north on McDaniel. As he passed the funeral home his car lit up in a shower of bullets and he drove erratically forward, accelerating to get away. The next intersection was blocked ahead and to the left, corralling him to go right towards a dead end into the railroad tracks. He gunned it down Gardner to make it to the next intersection to take Smith. Turning left on Smith his driver window exploded as a Great Dane leaped through biting into his shoulder and pulling him from the car which crashed through the fence and met with a tree at the Overcoming Church. The massive Dane dropped him bleeding on the road. Delarius pulled up behind him in his El Dorado, several other cars surround him.

Delarius exits the El Dorado and walks up to Marcus who is panting and bleeding profusely onto the street. Delarius stands above him with several more men behind him. "What say cuz? I hear you got a new plug. We havin' a talk about that." Delarius walks back to his El Dorado as Marcus is lifted into another vehicle and they head south on Smith.

They drove to a house on Garibaldi and push Marcus within. The music is blaring and Marcus is dizzy with adrenalin and loss of blood. He's seated kneeling on the floor with the two Great Danes standing watch before him. Delarius enters and falls into the couch across from him. "He say anything yet?" Delarius leans forward on the couch, never looking Marcus in the eye, but instead keeping his focus on the floor in front of him.

"Carriage Springs III apartments in Clarkston. Apartment 103."

"When?"

"Four am."

Delarius rose up from the couch and stood over Marcus blocking the light from the kitchen. "This better be right Marcus or I sweat to God boy!"

Idalia stepped into the church's meeting room on her way to the kitchen with a basket of okra, beans, and early tomatoes, smiling to Damien as she went by.

The self esteem class being taught by Simone continued as Idalia stepped around and into the kitchen.

Damien watched her through the open door as she sorted the vegetables, his concentration ever on her even as he looked away to Simone. He came to the Walking Together church center every opportunity he was afforded in hopes that she would be there. Usually she was, her dedication to helping and her love for nature and now especially gardening brought her here almost every day, even when no one else was at the center. He had come before to find the center locked only to see Idalia behind working in the garden. He had been afraid to approach her and instead sat quietly, for as long as he dared, watching her as she worked, only leaving for fear she might see him.

In fact she had seen him and it had made her uneasy. She was happy to see him getting help and the improvement in his color was apparent as his nutrition improved through so much fresh food from her garden.

Damien had been lost in thought as Jacob arrived at Walking Together and he felt a surge of white panic when he looked back to Idalia to see her arms wrapped around the boy. He had seen the two together before, but not with this intimacy. He felt his heartbeat accelerate and his breath quickened with a tightening in his chest and a desperate need to flee, so real, so urgent as if a wild animal were just three steps behind him. He pushed back in his chair and ran for the door, wrenching it open and casting himself desperately into the evening air. He gasped as tears rolled down his cheeks and he ran to the back of the church past the garden, pausing briefly to look at it and think again of her working there, calming him only so briefly. He heard the door of the church open and Elias calling his name. He ran on across the street and hid behind a large tree, curling himself up at the base of it and feeling nothing but his pain and self loathing. He had nothing he could offer to her. No way of making her see how much she meant to him. Outside her light his world was painted in the familiar hues of despair he had come to know so well through his life. His head pounded with emotion – pain, frustration, anger – a cacophony of maddening dread with no escape and no perceivable conclusion.

He pulled off his shoe and removed the needle wedged against the side of his foot. The tears rolled faster down his cheeks as he undid his shoelace and wrapped it around his arm. His hand shaking as he tried to aim the needle for the vein. The release came quickly, but it was muted. Heroin wasn't enough to combat his feelings of loss and devastation. He let it drop from his hand and pressed his face into both palms to push out the world.

He waited behind the tree as the evening continued on. The class concluded and he watched as everyone left, seeing Idalia for the briefest of moments as she drove by with Simone. At least Jacob wasn't with her. He calmed to a degree knowing they weren't still together. When he was certain the church was vacated, he went back to walk in her garden. Looking where he could see the step of her sandals in the soil, the impression of her hands into the dirt. At times he could find the imprint of her fingers and place his there as well. He caressed the plants and inhaled their smell which he associated with goodness and everything positive; but mostly with her. She grew here. Everything good grew here through her. This was the heart of all creation, where his soul resided. The green tomatoes, turning colors on their way to a deep red, were like to his own heart which she grew and nurtured here. He lay down again amidst the vegetation, heedless of the insects that crawled about him and the mosquitoes that fed from him. He wished himself to sink within the earth, his fingers and toes extending out roots and from his heart growing a great magnificent tree bearing every kind of fruit and vegetable, crowding out all the other plants in her garden so she had only this tree, his tree, to care and tend to. He pictured her sitting beneath his shade on a summer day, climbing up within his branches to reach olives, tomatoes, cucumbers, strawberries, apples, every sort of melon, an endless variety of abundance. He would respond to her every need and desire, pulling goodness from the sun, soil and rain to bursting forth a richness she would pick and eat directly from him as she sat amongst his branches. At night she would stay with him, sleeping upon his branches and he would keep her safe and warm always and forever.

The continuing bites of the mosquitoes reminded him he was still a man or some shadow of what could be called a man. He pulled himself up and stared back at the church. Inside he was hollow. Like the rind of an acorn squash, there was nothing he had to offer her, nothing she would see as genuine worth within him as there was absolutely nothing. A dark, eternal field of barren black where not even an echo feeds back. It swallows everything and gives nothing in return, for nothing sates its appetite for goodness. An entire universe of purity and light it could envelop in a moment without the briefest of brightening or a minute interruption from immortal silence. Damien dug his fingers into the soil before him, churning it as his breathing shuddered and his face grew tense and red. He held his breath and clawed deep, wishing to dig himself down, and let out a desperate agonized cry, rich with sorrow, layered with remorse and utterly without hope.

He felt the snap with that cry from the delicate thread that this place, this church, this garden and that girl managed to hold him from a fall back to madness. They didn't care, she certainly didn't care, how could she? Why should she? Care for what? Roadkill? He was alone, these feelings hadn't been real. The only reality for him was pain. Pain and heroin, they defined who he was and there was nothing further. These recent feelings, however pleasant they had appeared, were illusory. They were fickle. They had no permanence and were no match for the stagnancy of the void that filled him. It was a lie, a cruel hoax played just to mock him. Before he knew it he took one of the unripe tomatoes beside him and tore it from the vine casting it angrily at the back of the church. A pair of crows sat on the roof watching as he did this. He wanted to feel remorse for this, but instead he grabbed another and another and another heaving them with all his might. He stood up and walked back into the garden pushing over the bean poles and lashing out at the corn stalks. He pulled up a melon still connected to its vine and sent it crashing to the ground bursting open and then stomping upon it, tears streaming down his face and saliva seeping from his open agonized mouth. He ran from the garden, his body heaving in deep grieving cries as he ran off into the night.

The El Dorado pulled up with its deep guttural thrum and cut the lights. Opening the door he steps out in his trademark crocodile boots and slipped the Glock behind his back into his belt. He lifted the seat back to let his two danes out and then shut the door with a slam, watching the door of apartment 103 in front of him for any reaction. There were no lights on. He glanced briefly to his left to see his heavies parked nearby awaiting the signal. He preferred to start the introduction himself, confident in his ability to negotiate through intimidation first and violence later.

He straighten up and cracked his neck, rolling his shoulders and pumping himself up. He walked a brisk pace to the door and, tensing up, kicked it in with a single blow from his right foot. The danes ran within barking fiercely, the door rebounding back to close again. He kicked it in again and walked inside, his left hand holding the Glock still in the back of his jeans. The danes were still barking, but occasionally whimpered and the darkness of the room left Delarius wondering if anyone was there. He could make out a swirl of smoke and then the red glow as someone inhaled on a cigarette from a chair ten feet in front of him.

The danes settled down and stared, growling, intently at the smoking figure. Delarius took the opportunity to light up himself, not to be intimidated by his undetermined adversary.

"Happy you were able to find the place." Tyco spoke through the smoke he exhaled from his chair.

Delarius fought to remain at ease. He was unfamiliar with his aggression tactics coming up short and had to recalibrate his thoughts in ordered to best proceed.

"You sent Marcus out as bait?"

"Not bait, more a request for a meeting. Its about time we get to know each other don't you think?"

Delarius felt his mind fog with outrage and absent mindedly withdrew the pistol from his belt to hold it in his left hand aggressively. "Who the fuck do think you are making requests of me, huh?" The danes growled again. A curious laughing began from the darkness in front of him. The danes tensed and backed up with great unease. Delarius could just make out flickers of animal eyes shining out at him. "What the fuck is that?" He pointed the pistol at the eyes. The danes were still backing up as they growled, their eyes doing a much better job of sizing up the threat before them than Delarius. "I swear to got, you tell that thing to back up right the fuck now!"

"Frankly son, I don't know how the hell to tell these bitches what to do. They do their thing is all."

"I will shoot those fucking dogs right now motherfucker! I ain't playin' with you, get those sons of bitches away from you right goddam now!"

The laughter continued and the danes, one giving out a final bark, rushed out of the apartment into the street, only there to continue barking unceasingly, hoping to keep the threat at bay and convince Delarius to leave that place.

The two beasts in the shadows stopped their laughing and their eyes went dark. For all Delarius knew they had retreated to a back room. He realized he had been breathing heavily and quickly and he he worked to focus and calm himself back down. He chose to put the gun back in his belt. The danes kept barking behind him making it difficult for him to think. "Shut up!" He cried over his shoulder and they sat down and whimpered, looking in the door waiting for him. "Now we can have a civilized conversation about this. Let's start with who the fuck you are coming into my town with your shit?" Delarius felt immediately from the silence that his antagonist had fled.

He went to the door and whistled to the waiting car. It opened and the men ran out to him. "Rashaun, get in there and sweep this place. Y'all drive around and make sure he ain't snuck out the back. Motherfucker!"

Simone and Idalia unloaded the vegetables Idalia had brought from the church garden into the house. Memphis stood upon the couch watching them, Idalia running her hand across the cat as she passed.

"My point Doll is, Damien's not showing the ability to focus when you are around. Well, he's focusing, but his focus is on you. He might or might not have the real desire to improve his situation, but his actions tonight make it clear he's idolizing you." Simone placed the basket of beans and okra on the counter and turned to face Idalia who looked intently back to her. "And that's not acceptable."

"I know and I agree with you."

"You've helped him a great deal, but the level of interest he's showing you is dangerous. Obsession is an unpredictable thing."

"I really wanted to see him get better."

"And you did. He did get better, much better. But he can't get better by constructing unrealistic hopes and dreams around you." Simone ran her fingers through Idalia's hair. "I'll make sure someone is taking good care of him sweetie, its just important he gets his help elsewhere."

Idalia went to her room and nestled into her bed with The Blizzard by Pushkin given to her by Jacob to read.

Simone came and knocked on her door. "Doll, I'm going out for a bit, I should be back by 10 or 11 okay?"

"Okay. Be careful."

"Give me a call if you need anything okay?"

"I will."

Idalia continued with the story, pausing on occasion to make a note in her journal from a thought that approached her.

A tap at her window drew her attention. She sees a robin perched outside the sill. The bird fluffs its feathers and continues staring forward into her room, tapping occasionally as if to be let in. Idalia laughs and places the book down, going to the window and tapping back to chase the bird off. The bird doesn't flee but continues to tap and chirp. Tickled, Idalia unlatches and opens the window. The robin flies within and circles the room chirping its away until landing atop the mirror above her dresser.

"Hello there!" She puts her hands on her hips and stares up at the bird on its new perch. "Making yourself at home?"

The robin chirps several times again loudly. Idalia hears Memphis scratching at the door to her room. She normally spends the night sleeping with her, but with her new roommate she feels this is ill advised.

"Not sure how this arrangement is going to – " Her words are cut short with a shout as she's grabbed from behind. She struggles as the assailant holds her firmly back against them with one arm and place a rag soaked in a sharp strong liquid in the other. She claws at the hands that bind her struggling not to breath, kicking and pushing away. They fall together against the bed and then to the floor, her assailant placing their weight against her harshly to bind her. She tries to scream but can only cry as she weakens. She wishes for Jacob, Simone anyone to help her as she sobs and slips to unconsciousness.

A full moon hung isolated in the night sky. A rabbit foraged below amidst the wreckage of Idalia's garden, its ears perking up at the approach of several vehicles. A sedan and a Chevy pickup with a trailer pulled into the Walking Together church parking lot just after 2:30am. Seven men stepped out of the vehicles along with Pascal. The group split in two, some heading for the church basement door and the others drove the Chevy into the garden and plowing through the hedge into the clearing. They jumped out with shovels and in the midst of the clearing they set to work digging.

Pascal kicked in the door to the church basement until it gave way and the went inside. Moving tables and chairs from their path they pulled back the area rug in the midst of the room to uncover the large stone set within the tiling at the center of the room. Pascal and the others each took a pick axe and began to break up the flooring surrounding the stone. Using crowbars and shovels they pried the seven foot long stone from the floor, gaining a hold on it and standing it up on its side. They rested it on a small dolly they brought and wheeled it out of the church basement.

The second group began striking a solid object with their shovels and similarly began to wedge a second stone out of the earth. They lifted it up into the trailer and circled the Chevy around the clearing and back across the devastated garden to park beside the other stone which was heaved upon its sibling. Pascal rushed back out of the church basement and into the truck which then took off down the road, the sedan following. As the vehicles receded in the distance the glow of flames became more apparent from within the church basement.

The unmitigated sense of panic that had consumed him upon arriving at the hospital was converted to incompressible fury. His eyes felt hot, his teeth clenched; burning tears streaming down his face as he paced the hall outside her room. Simone was still inside holding Idalia's hand as she rested. He pounded his fist against the wall and heaved three deep sobs knocking his forehead as he moaned in his pain. It was Damien, he was sure of it. The doctor said she had been drugged. Damien must have fled when Simone returned before he could harm her any further. They were clearing the drugs from her system and giving her something to recover from the trauma of the attack.

Damien was going to pay. He was going to make him pay deeply for this.

He rushed out of the hospital, no thought of letting Simone know where he was going. His mind was a frenzy of activity. He droves his car back to his apartment and threw open the door. "Dad!" He raced around the rooms for his father, but he was not to be found.

He sits on the bed with his head in his hands, the thumping of his blood making him dizzy. Concentrate! He jumps back up and races to his car, leaving the apartment door wide open in his haste. He drives madly through the night to the homeless shelter. He pounds on the door demanding to be let him. Someone finally opens it slight. "Please let me in, I need to speak to Elias, it's an emergency!"

The person at the door looks at him for a minute and ascertaining the urgency is no joke. "Hold on a minute." He closes the door and Jacob waits impatiently, pacing about on the sidewalk. After ten minutes the door reopens and Elias steps out groggily rubbing his eye. "Jacob? What's all the ruckus?"

"Damien, he attacked Doll. She's in the hospital recovering."

"Good Lord! Is she alright?"

"I – I don't know. I think so. Simone is with her and I think she is okay. He fucking drugged her Elias." By this time Jacob could not control his tears and he shuddered as they ran through him. Elias had never heard him swear before, but that was the least of the marvels happening to him at this hour.

"Okay okay son, did you call the police?"

"Yeah, yeah Simone did when she got home and found her. Elias you've got to help me find him!"

"Wait, hold on! That is not a good idea."

117

"Fuck good ideas! I need to see his face right now and know why he did this to her! I need your help, I know you can tell me where he'd be."

"Now I've been cleaned for years. I don't know where he gets his fix."

"That's bullshit and you know it!" Jacob tried to calm down. "Look, Elias, I know you've stayed clean, but I also know you keep tabs on what's out there. No one's going to hurt me in some crack house, I just want to get to Damien before its too late and he gets away. I know he'd need a fix after what he did."

"Son, I don't know what to tell you. Its best to leave this to the police —"

"I'm sick of not doing anything. I'm sick of coming home to my dad passed out on the floor. I'm sick of these people ruining my life!"

"Jacob, its —"

"Elias, just shut up, you're coming with me." He grabbed the old man by the arm and pulled him to his car. Once inside he turned to Elias again. "Now, which way?"

Elias knew exactly where Damien would be. There was only one place he could be on this night and they pulled up in front of the abandoned prison off of Keys Road. There were no other vehicles around. They stepped out and Elias led the way through the burned out remains of large building now open to the sky and littered with charred and rusted detritus.

They continued through the grass and trees to a smaller structure still standing. Entering within they felt the stillness of quiet addicts sprawled out all about them, each projected to a place unconnected to their fragile physical form. Jacob accidentally stepped on the hand of a woman and she gave no reaction at all. He searched for Damien among the living corpses surrounding him on the floor, aiming his flashlight into their faces and moving quickly on to the next until with a shock he saw the face of his father.

His face was sickly pale. The eyes didn't react to the light, but were reacting as if to something else they were experiencing far from here. He shook him, "Dad! Wake up dad, its Jacob! Dammit dad!" His face knotted up and blood ran red to it. "Why are you like this dad? What is your problem?" He began to cry again. His father gave no reaction to him, just silently breathing at a pace that seems too low to sustain him and staring at his far off experience.

Elias left him to his suffering, hoping it might distract him from the search for Damien. In fact Elias had already found Damien comatose in the next room. He'd moved some stale old newspapers over him in hopes that Jacob would overlook him. Damien only had one shoe and the third toe on the exposed foot was badly fracture and thrusting out of order gruesomely. He heard footsteps approaching coming into the room where Jacob sat with his father. Elias' heart began to race and he hid against the wall not wanting the police or any dealer to catch him here.

Jacob heard the steps as well and looked up as Tyco entered the room, his flashlight beamed directly on Jacob blinding him. He walked over towards Jacob and a crow flew in a shattered window above. Suddenly the room was bright as a band of cars pulled up outside the building and they could hear doors quickly opening and closing. Tyco drew his weapon and ran for cover. Jacob looked around in confusion of what to do next. Leave his father and hide himself? Before he could decide two Great Danes came rushing into the room and stopped before him growling in the dark. He backed up to the wall from them and they inched closer. "Elias!" He called out but got no answer. Elias was already out the back of the building running across fields to get away.

Delarius and a group of his men entered, the tell-tale sound of his boots laying a soundtrack for the early morning's schedule. He walked up past the danes and grabbed Jacob by his chin to make him look Delarius in the eye. "Now who the fuck would you be?"

"No one, I was just looking for my dad." Jacob struggled to maintain his dignity and talk while Delarius continued to firmly hold his face.

"Daddy." Delarius looked at the man sprawled out on the floor beside them, "That your daddy?"

"Yes."

Delarius stared intently deciding what he thought of this answer. He was told by a snitch that his nemesis with the crazy dogs would be here tonight. So far he'd only found junkies and one straight ass kid. He let go of Jacob and the dogs followed him back to his men who had been searching the rooms. Tyco had already snuck out the back and was keeping an eye on things from a safer distance.

"Check the area, maybe we spooked him." Delarius sent his crew out to look while the danes accompanied him inside. He came back around to Jacob. "Mr Daddy's Boy. What's your name Daddy's Boy?"

"Jacob."

"Jacob." He paced around some more, looking. "Jacob you come here all by yourself looking for your daddy?"

"Yes sir."

Delarius laughed, "And how is it you knew where to find him precisely?"

"Another junkie told me where to look."

"Another junkie. And where might that other junkie be now?"

"I don't know, I just asked him where to look is all."

"He didn't want to, uh, come with you for his own fix then?"

"No sir, he's cleaned up."

"Cleaned up!" More laughter at this. "He cleaned himself up, but he still knows where the good shit is going down. That sounds like a true junkie to me."

"Tell me Jacob, and I want you to be honest with me." Delarius walked up close to the boy. "Have you seen anyone else here tonight other than these fucking bootless junkies?"

Jacob thought about Elias and hoped he had gotten far away from here. He also thought about the man who'd hidden when the lights of the cars shown in the place. He wondered if he should bring it up. He wondered what might happen to him if he didn't bring it up. "Uh, there was someone here, but he left when he saw the cars."

Delarius perked up at this. "Which way did he leave?"

Jacob point to the right where he had seen Tyco run to hide.

"Just one guy?"

"Yes."

Delarius left with the danes and shouted out orders to more thoroughly search the area. Jacob watched as he left and was surprised when and arm went over his mouth with a wet caustic cloth. He fought with his assailant and kicked out against the wall, striking and knocking is father over in his strain. With his other arm the man struck Jacob's leg behind the knee with a blunt bat and Jacob dropped to the floor while the assailant pinned him down until he'd breathed enough through the cloth to lose consciousness.

Pascal worked Jacob up, heaved him over his shoulder and began heading out of the building.

"Don't you move motherfucker!" Rashaun shouted at him, his pistol pointed at Pascal as he crossed the room towards him. Pascal paused to consider him briefly before a hyena came from behind and knocked Rashaun to the floor. His gun went off and Pascal continued with his burden towards an exit. With a single bite the beast tore off Rashaun's shoulder and neck leaving him to quake and bleed across the floor.

The sounds of cackling laughter could be heard in the distance as the hyena raced around the building. Pascal kept his pace with Jacob on his way to his Lexus. Shots rang out at him and one struck him in the arm. He kept going on adrenaline and ignored the bite and shock of it. Delarius called the danes on him, but he still never turned. They would overtake him before he reached the car and Delarius laughed with anticipation. The danes raced at full speed and Delarius shot over their heads, not aiming just taunting Pascal. They narrowed the field quickly, preparing the ambush to bring him down, only to be hit by the hyena from the side in surprise. The hyena took down the first dane and leaped up to chase after the second which tried to outdistance it. The cries of a second hyena could plainly be heard now on the far side of the building along with gunfire and mad screams of terror and agony. Pascal reached the Lexus and threw Jacob within. Delarius fired more shots and shattered the back window as the car charged down the dirt road and away.

He went over in shock to the Great Dane. Its chest was heaving and the eyes bulged out as it looked up at him. It was unable to get up, the hyena had ripped a great hole in its stomach and a dislocated hind leg hung loosely behind it now. As he caressed the failing beast he could hear the death shriek of his second dane off in the distance.

Tyco was celebrating in his house on Fairview Street as the dawn began to make its way. He had two of his finest bitches with him in the hot tub and cocktails flowing from the backyard bar. With Delarius out of the picture, he felt he owned Atlanta. Milledgeville seemed like a cruel joke to him now when he looked at what he had achieved since then. He lifted himself out of the water and sat on the edge of the tub, motioning for the girls. One went behind him to massage his shoulders and the other went down on his cock and worked her magic with her lips.

"Oh Lord slow down baby, we got all the time in the world today." He grabbed the back of her head and shoved her deeper down his shaft and held her there for a moment before letting her go to cough and resume her smooth slow devotion.

He sang along with the Curtis Mayfield song playing "Two can be one for the righteous way to go…anyone would know –"

A bullet shot through his shoulder and hit the leg of the girl behind him. She let out a scream as did the second girl who swam to hide on at the far side of the hot tub. Tyco fell to his back holding his shoulder and feeling the hot blood coursing over his fingers. The girl who'd be shot was still crying heavily behind him repeating "Oh God! Oh Jesus! I'm dying!"

Delarius and his remaining men surrounded Tyco triumphantly. Delarius pointed his pistol at Tyco's shrunken penis, "Look at that little dick on this motherfucker." He looked at the girl still in the pool. "You get that thing stuck between your teeth when you suckin' that shit? Damn boy, that is one sorry ass prick." And with that Delarius fired two bullets through Tyco's genitals.

Jacob woke on a couch with a throbbing headache. The room kept spinning as he sat up and he had to pause for fear he would throw up. It was too late, he heaved his guts upon the floor in front of him. The contractions continued into dry heaves once his stomach had not even bile to offer. He fell back against the couch exhausted, his vision blurring in and out of near focus to double or triple images. He wanted to fall back asleep more than anything. He pressed his face into the couched and breathed in the smell of it. Then the nausea returned and he had just enough energy to lean forward and heave the smallest of bile dripping from his open mouth as he flexed and gagged in exhausted agony. He panted and moaned from the pain and exhaustion. Wishing for it to stop and let him rest. Someone placed crackers, cheese and soda water in front of him. He could not focus on who it was though he felt he needed to, instead he went for the soda water and drank it slowly holding his head in his right hand. He took his time with it, concentrating on keeping it down and recovery. Eventually he got some crackers down as well, but decided the cheese was far too much for him. With half the soda water gone, he finally felt exhaustion take hold of him again.

The next time he awoke, he felt improvement. It was late afternoon and dusk would be coming soon. The headache was a soft throb of what it had once been. He looked up around him with eyes that now could focus and unify objects into a single image. Ceiling, wall, window, glass door. He slowly sat up. Outside the window was fields of green, a barn, a truck with a trailer. The sky was ominous in the distance, portend to an approaching storm. He was on a farm, this much was clear. Why this was the case he had no comprehension of. He raised himself to his feet and went to the glass door. Before he could open it he heard the laughter. It startled him as it came from behind him to the left. He turned to see a hyena watching him with its dead cold eyes. The beast was huge, but silent when not laughing. He could not even see the motion of its breath on its chest. He was certain, however, that it was not allowing him to open that door.

He went back to the couch and glanced around the rest of the room to see if he might have other options. There was a hallway to the left. He decided to slowly make he way towards it and see what reaction that might merit. The beast allowed him passage and he hurried his pace some. There was a front door up ahead and he started to run towards it, working the lock and pulling it quickly open. The hyena stood before him outside the door staring through him with the deadness of coal.

Shutting the door he heard a familiar buzz somewhere nearby. He searched frantically about the room, turning over magazines, books, old notebooks, piles of clothing and then found his cell phone. The battery was failing but he had enough to send a text to Simone.

Delarius drove the El Dorado without music, nothing but the roar of the engine and the drum of the rain on the roof to accompany him. His danes were dead. He never let anyone else ride in the car with him, not even his finest pussy. His posse followed behind him in seven other cars. Heavily armed. Ready for a showdown.

Tyco had folded gracefully once his manhood was shot off. If he'd had more time on his hands he would have fed that shit to him. But this thought only upset him further. His true wish would have been to feed it to his danes. He was going to get this son-of-a-bitch for what he'd done. This was beyond war. This was retribution of the highest order.

They turned off the main road to a dirt road that led to the farm. Things were about to go quickly. First things first he was gonna kill those goddam bitches that butchered his dogs. He could see the farm ahead of him, few lights on and masked by the sheets of water fervently pelting all to be seen. He accelerated, the farm house was in front of him now and he pushed straight for it. As he did, a hyena stepped into his path and he pressed his pedal to the floor screaming obscenities through a frothing mouth. The beast took one step towards him and leaped over his hood to land upon the roof and bound off once again. He slammed the breaks and spun wildly in the mud to turn in pursuit. The vehicle behind him had received the beast and its front window was smashed in. The car careened madly and Delarius worked to avoid it, spinning erratically through the slick Georgia mud. The hyena mauled the driver and the other occupants fired fervently into the creature. The car spun itself sideways into a tree and gun fire continued less frequently as the whole thing shook and rocked with the screams of desperate voices.

A spotlight flashed from a police truck and shone up the scene. The approach of the truck had been masked by the cacophony of storm, screams and gunfire. Delarius spun his car around once more and raced around the farmhouse. Jumping out, he ran to the glass back door and took a metal lawn table to it. Entering through the shattered glass with his pistol drawn he looked for the asshole who'd killed his dogs. Entering the living room he found Jacob and fired, just missing him as Jacob dove to the floor. He fired again, but the second hyena leaped in his aim taking the bullet. Delarius drew very still as he saw it flex for a final leap towards him. He screamed out in blood rage and fired several more shots into its chest and face as the monster grabbed him with its front paws by the waist locking its jaws around his shoulder pulled him cleanly in half.

Jacob took the moment to rush for the door and into the mayhem of the torrential night. The first hyena was still massacring the occupants of the car. The other vehicles had chosen to turn around and leave, but were barred by the arrival of a dozen police vehicles flashing and squealing their sirens to join the fray. The truck continued to light the scene and report the bedlam. Jacob ran off towards the woods, the hyena ravaging the last souls in the car thrusting itself repeatedly at the car door when it saw him. He ran faster than he ever had, pushing his limits and gritting his jaw for maximum air. He knew it was impossible with the speed of that animal, but was desperate for his freedom. Lights appeared erratically in his path and he saw Simone's BMW racing towards him over the rough field. She pulled it to a stop in front of him and jumped out to rush to him. She began swinging something above her head, it made a soothing tone. "Get in the car!" He cried warning to her, knowing the beast must be right on his tail. She grabbed his arm vigorously and held him against her as she swung the silver device around them both. He turned to see that both hyenas had approached them but kept clear of the swinging charm. She held her free arm around him and walked them back to the car slowly, swinging the entire time. Jacob was unsure if it was the liquid within the charm or the rain that was spraying out of it. The hyenas kept their distance, but followed as closely as this circle of protection would allow them.

"Jacob open the car door!" Simone screamed and he did so. He crawled across to the passenger side and she stood in the rain swinging the wailing charm through the air. She dialed her phone with her free arm, her eyes never off the two beasts.

"Yes this is an emergency! This is Simone Cartwright. I am at the farm on 92 Wilcof Road in Alpharetta Georgia. I have the boy Jacob in my white BMW 325i license plate ACR 428. He is safe at unharmed. I am about to come back towards the officers, we are being pursued by two large animals from the farm and desperately need assistance. No, I – I can't hold on I have to move now. Just let officer Crenshaw know its Simone in the BMW and he needs to take down these two animals now." She waited a few more minutes swinging the silver charm through the air, but slowly its tone changed shape and the hyenas became more tense and prepared, as if expectant that this impediment could only continue so much longer. She swung harder, her arm growing stiff from the effort, though she had thrice changed hands for relief. Finally she let it fly and dove inside the vehicle, putting it in reverse and slamming her foot into the gas. They spun nothing but mud for a moment and the hyenas charged them, but finally the car caught hold and began driving back. Simone held the back of Jacob's seat and looked behind them aiming her car towards the dirt road and the police cars still stationed there. Most had gone up to the farm, but some where still keeping a lookout back at the end of the farm road. Jacob stared at the hyenas. They effortlessly kept pace with the car and looked to be closing the distance. She sped faster, the engine racing in reverse. They bounced over holes, rotting logs and rocks but she kept it on course towards the road. The BMW shone its light on the scene making the brutal beasts feel even more at hand in their hurtling charge. He looked behind him to see three of the police cars on intercept with them. Simone drive through their midst and they closed in front of her to block the hyenas. The creatures vaulted the vehicles and kept up the chase. A police van raced back down the road and Simone spun the BMW behind it as she finally reached the driveway and shifted into first. The demon dogs leaped to the top of the van and sailed down to her car, the first missing it by mere feet and the second landing on the hood, its claws scraping into the metal and fighting for a grip. She pushed first to its maximum and slipped into second with the same force, the beast tumbled off, but they both kept up their pursuit. The engine, hot with enthusiasm, began to pressure their hunt and she roughly bounced off the dirt path onto pavement revving ever faster and harder as the distance widen between them.

Pascal charged the Chevy truck down 400 into Atlanta. He felt levity in the air. Everything was going according to his expectations. There was no stopping the inevitable now. 150 years of anticipation were culminating in the next 24 hours. Nothing was left to chance. There was no wrong move left to make. He charged down through Atlanta on his way to Milledgeville.

He forged his truck down the long dirt road. He tingled with excitement. The air was crisp, still heavy with the recent rain and his heart pounded within him. He pulled past the main house and behind the barn and drove out into the open overgrown field behind. Sound left the scenery as history filled his mind. He felt that moment so very long ago now when his life was draining from him right here.

He slammed the brakes, breathing heavily, his hands shaking as they stiffly gripped the wheel. Leaping from the truck he unlatched the back of the trailer and looked upon the two stones. Each now emitted a glow, dull but apparent. They no longer felt like stone and their dense weight had abandoned them. Easily he pulled them off and positioned them to his own remembered specifications upon the wet grass. He stood between them, marveling at their inherent beauty, still after all this time uncertain of their real power and purpose. In the dark trees above a pair of crows watched the night's events with interest.

He entered the mansion and prepared himself for the inevitable engagement to come. A curious sound and dim light issued from one of the side rooms and he entered it. A woman lay on a hospital bed, equipment monitoring her state. She looked in absolute peace. She was breathtaking. He remembered his own wife and began to choke up. He stroked her dark beautiful hair and spent a moment watching her breath. Compelled, he kissed her gently on the forehead and held her hand briefly before returning to his preparations for the night's affairs. He went directly down into the cellar. Grabbing an axe he began to break up the hard soil floor. The dusty floor smelt of age, rot and mold. He took off his shirt and wrapped it over his mouth and nose and continued to work at the floor. It gave way in chunks, sometimes fighting, sometimes yielding freely. He worked a large section of the floor deeper and deeper below until he began to strike iron. He worked his way across an area over six foot in length and four in width steadily ringing out the sound of the iron below the surface. Once it was appropriately exposed he dusted about until he found a rusted handle and wrenched at it with the sum of his might. He used the axe to strike the edge of the iron crate he'd exposed until the lid freed itself with a hop. Gripping the handle once more he pried with a cry and cast the lid open.

With a cold impassive air, Bast the great lioness leapt out of her interminable crypt.

Pascal drove his truck down to the Milledgeville cemetery breaking through the chain that kept it closed after hours. He traveled to the Mausoleum of Aquilla. Proud and singular in its grandeur, the bright moon overhead appeared as a spotlight upon it, pouring intense shadows from the structure that beckoned Pascal to hasten. Shadows flashed above as a body of crows landed among the nearby trees. He took the axe he had brought and hacked away the chain on the mausoleum door, dragging it open on its rusty hinges. Inside was the stone coffin of Aquilla, moonlight slashing across it through the barred windows from above. He pushed on the heavy stone lid, but it was too much for him to move on his own. He again turned to the axe and swung recurrently against its center until the piece cracked in two. He pushed off these two pieces and stared down at the corpse, pausing just a moment as his breath ceased. There was no sign of death, no sign that time had passed. The corpse had simply waited for his arrival. Waited for this night. He lifted the great dead man out and over his shoulder, pulling him out to the truck and dropping him onto the trailer bed, driving the body back to the plantation where he had last seen life 150 years before.

Idalia leapt in Jacob's arms as he entered the hospital room she had been waiting in. Tears streamed down her as she kissed him repeated across every inch of his face, his eyes and again and again to his lips, whose texture and generosity dissolved the painful world away in an ecstasy of adoration and unassailable refuge. "Are you okay my darling?"

Jacob pulled her tight against her. "I'm with you my love. I'm with you."

Simone waited as patiently as she could for the pair to share a moment before beckoning them to follow her. They went down to the garage and entered the battered and ravaged BMW. Idalia clung to Jacob appealing for details of what madness had beset them while she had waited for their return. Simone interrupted, "Doll dear." She ran her fingers through Idalia's hair. "We'll have time for that later. Right now we all need to rest and help each other recover. Please, both of you get in the back of the car. We're going somewhere safe."

"We're not going home?"

"No Doll, not until we hear from the police. I'm taking you both somewhere I know you can't be hurt. I love you so much my sweet. Now please, get in the car. Let's go."

They entered the car and Idalia cuddled up against Jacob who wrapped his arms tightly about her, shunning the madness of the world in a blanket of pure tenderness.

Simone pulled the car out of the parking lot and headed towards the interstate. "Here Doll." She handed back a thermos to Idalia. "Drink some tea both of you so you can relax. We will be there soon and I want you both to be able to get some sleep."

Pascal pulled back up the path into the plantation. The crows in the moonlit trees stared down as he passed. They stood on the roof of the mansion and on the barns, all silently watching. Even more sinisterly, bats now hung from branches and wheeled about in the sky above him in great numbers. He pulled into the overgrown field and saw torches lit and placed around the area he'd lain the stones. Various dogs stood watch in the field, some looking wild others looking purebred. They watched his approach. A scurry of large black rats made way as the truck came to a stop. Before the stones two men and a woman stood dressed in white tunics staring blankly as his vehicle approached. At the side they had set Daphne, still unconscious and still on her hospital bed. Behind them was an assembly of six beings of various dress, one with no dress and but half of a man holding itself upright by its arms. Its gruesome face jawless and eyeless. The gods of old he knew, come to await the final act. Pascal exited the vehicle and viewed the ineluctable progress of the preordained eventualities. Nothing was left to chance. So much has been riding for so long on this night, the air felt it would crack with the deafening silence of oppressive anticipation.

A monkey stood upon the shoulder of the tallest of the men. It stared at him with a thinking mind unlike the dogs, unlike the crows, unlike the hyenas or Bast. This beast seemed to know his purpose, his mind, his intentions. It contemplated them, concerned itself with his capacities, his potential for misfortune. The wind turned suddenly and the smoke from the torches blew towards him, their odor distinct, flashing colorful memories to his mind of exotic places, burning passions and achingly satisfying levels of suffering. The monkey leapt from the shoulder of the man to avoid the smoke and the dogs nearest the stones and the torches that surrounded them backed away until the wind receded.

Pascal went to the trailer and lowered its gate to reveal the corpse. The men came to his aid and they carried the body of Aquilla over to lay him across the leftmost stone. Its glow was unworldly, seeming to shape the air surrounding it. As they laid the corpse upon it, Pascal felt a duplicity of time and experience. A distance too vast to conquer with the human mind. A meaning unfathomable, yet enticing.

He knew it was a risk to leave the stones and the torches that lit about them. The dogs could easily rip him apart now he had nothing left to bargain his life for. But he did not believe Mephisto truly grasped his role, his intention in this morbid undertaking. The beast was cognizant of certain truths, but wrestled at the nature of intention. He exited the protective circle and approached Mephisto, who sat perched staring at him from the back of his truck. He walked up to the monkey and they stared into each other's eyes for a time, neither able to descry the truth of the other's nature. He opened the truck and lifted a bag from the back seat. Stripping all his clothes and opened the bag and pulled out a white tunic when he placed upon himself.

A van approached and stopped beside his truck. Adrik stepped from this. Pascal could see bound figures through the windows of the van and knew these were inmates of Central State Hospital. This was precisely the potentiality he had anticipated for some time.

Simone's battered BMW came to a stop behind his trailer. The chessboard was fully set.

Simone stepped from the car and approached Pascal, her eyes wide with both anger and fascination. He let her contemplate him for some time until she spoke, "There is no way I've been able to fathom who or what you are."

Pascal let her stare on him in silence for another moment. He glanced into the car where Jacob and Idalia slept in each other's arms. "I think you know quite well who I am and why I am here."

Her eyes contemplated this briefly and her mouth went firm with emotion. "If that is the case, why are you obstructing us?"

Pascal turned from her to Mephisto and then to the gowned duo near the stones. "Why am I obstructing you? Why do you think I was ever obstructing you? I was securing the outcome that has been designated for a long time."

"As are we, have you not seen the care and vigilance we have maintained all these years?"

"I have no quarrel with your commitment to this sacrament, my concern was your true motivations after all this time. Would they have maintained their initial purity of intention, or had any of you felt the pull towards personal sanctity?"

"The sacrament is nearly complete, why would we risk the complexity of initiating something completely new without an ordained and when our realization was finally so close at hand?" She stripped as she asked this, for time was short and her concerns had waned through the discussion. She adorned herself in her own tunic.

"You have only but one opportunity to become a god in this lifetime. Tonight is that night." She looked at him as he finished these words.

"As you see, I brought the two, not seventeen."

"And yet this van comes filled with lunatics."

It was true what he said. She had to think quickly for a proper answer but was not prepared. Adrik stepped in.

"As you said, we only have tonight, we could not take chances if the procedure were to fail. They are simply here as a fallback."

The moon was nearing the apex of its ascent in the cloudless sky. Simone and the other cult members carefully drew the two drugged children from the car and carried them to the second stone, undressing them and clothing them in similar tunics.

Adrik revealed a larger version of the distinctive tool Pascal had used on the crows to turn one of them from life to unlife. Using a mallet he hammered this through the chest of Aquilla's corpse so that its forked ends surrounded the heart. It sung out as the points pierced into the stone below and the note carried onward in a beautiful reverberation. The stone grew brighter as the sound continued. A light breeze swirled through the area spinning the scented torch smoke around to create a sensual feel in the air. They each lapped of a bowl of dark brew and lifting the children up poured some down them as well. Simone offered it to Pascal, but he retrieved a bottle of his own elixir from the truck and drank heavily from this instead. Adrik injected some into Daphne via a syringe as Basilio, dressed in his white tunic looked on. Still uncertain, still afraid, still hopeful this would bring her back to him. Another breeze darted through the scene and again they breathed heavily on the pungent smoke. Pascal's loins burned with hunger and his blood burned with anger, frustration and deep lust. He turned to Simone and slapped her heavily with the back of his hand. Her lip burst open and blood ran down her chin to dapple her white tunic. He grabbed her by the arm and threw her against the truck, ripping the bottom of her tunic and entering her from behind. She bit into his hand drawing blood and he punished her from behind. He grabbed her head with his other hand and beat her skull against the edge of the truck's bed and she moaned and accepted him deeper inside her. He lifted her in the air and carried her within the swirling flames of the torches, for the wind continued to pick up and address the area. The moon climbed every closer to its apex above them. He threw her to the ground beside the stones and entered her again forcing her to relinquish all she could for him. Beside them Adrik wrestled with another cloaked man holding him down and choking him, pulling harshly on his cock and slapping it along with his balls. He flipped the man over and spit on his anus pushing himself within and slapping the back of the man's head as he did so. Basilio, dazed from the potion, worked his way to Daphne. She was outside the circle. He kissed her hand saying her name tenderly, wishing her to return to him. The wind changed again and the torch smoke flowed over them just for a moment. Daphne gasped out, her back arching. Basilio's heart raced and he lifted her in his arms smothering her with his tears and kisses. She was in daze, unable to speak, holding him but not quite aware of anything including who she was. Around them the others labored in orgiastic bliss, each drawing blood from their lovers, each punishing each other with the deepest desire for pain and pleasure. During the frenzy, Adrik kept looking to Simone and she back to him. He watched as Pascal punished her from behind, his eyes closed in concentration, his grip on her firm and ungiving. Adrik grabbed another blade from the grass and leapt at Pascal,

129

his body partially going outside the circle of torches. Bast swung her mighty paw across him and he fell to the ground, his spine severed. He looked at Simone, her body still undulating back and forth to the incessant rhythm of Pascal's drive. He reached his hand out towards her, tears running down his face. She reached for him and held his hand tightly, her eyes welling up. Adrik passed and his grip on her faded. Pascal, oblivious of these events pulled her arms behind her to reach his climactic finish with a cry and stood up, still pumping cum across her back and he gasped for breath. Basilio looked on in horror at the fall of Adrik. He knew not what to do. He wanted to take Daphne away from this place if he could be sure they would not be attacked by the ferocious beasts that surrounded them.

Amidst the intoxicated smoke, Jacob and Idalia issued to some form of consciousness in which they were only aware of the body of the other. Hungrily they ran their hands across each other, hot with the same unstoppable passions that surrounded them. They felt themselves climbing skyward above the stars deep into the heavens with only the light of their bodies to shine. Jacob tore the tunic from her and fed upon her arching breasts and she cried in ecstasy as she grasped his cock in her hand. Desperately he thrust within her and she screamed out with pleasure. He held down her hands and she fought against him to reach up and bite at his chest. He felt himself building to a staggering climax and he moaned out as he pulled her face to his, kissing her deeply with all his passion and feeling her reciprocation. She clawed into his back as he thrust deeper and stronger within her, her nails digging deep and drawing blood. He climaxed in an explosion of sensation that tensed his body so hard he growled with the pain and bit into her lip as he felt all his pleasure for her flooding inside of her.

As Jacob arched in the final throws of supernal ecstasy, Simone drove the elaborate dagger she held through his back, pushing him towards Idalia to spear them both at once. Blood still dripped down her face and across her bare breasts, her eyes flashed in the flickering torchlight as she pressed desperately forward. Jacob caught his fall and pushed Idalia from beneath him to slide her from the stone. He fell on his side with the blades now running straight through him. He felt no pain and was only dimly aware of his surroundings. Pascal came up behind Simone and drove a knife into the back of her neck, using its handle to pull her back and toss her away from the stones to land gasping and gushing blood in the grass before the truck. Mephisto let out a scream and the wind howled up in a sudden roar, the torches either snuffing out or falling over to spill into the grass. The dogs leaped the gap that had kept them at bay and began snapping and clawing at Pascal. Just as suddenly Bast cleared the stones from behind and tore unsparingly through the dogs. The panther vaulted as Bast was still shredding the canines and Pascal fell back before it, saved only as Eshe grabbed it by the neck and pull it to the ground. The two hyenas had completed their nonstop run from Alpharetta and they both tore into the panther. The two remaining cult members rush Pascal swinging spears and knives at him. A spear pierced his side and he drew himself from it falling to the ground as he tripped over Idalia. They advanced upon him as Bast vaulted him and took them both down in a single massive gorge of blood and rent flesh. Bast turned once more to guard against the remaining dogs who in impossible desperation hoped to get past her fury to level their resentment upon Pascal. Bats swarmed from the sky and rats overwhelmed him as he fought ineffectively against them. He pushed Jacob's bleeding body from the Giving Stone. The boy fought for life still, with blood seeping from his nose and mouth. Beneath the stone he drew a sword and attempted to draw his lighter upon it when Narin grabbed him from behind and tossed him far from the circle. He prepared himself for the fall dropping the sword on his way to avoid impaling himself. But he did not fall, Bast caught him on his way down and brought in gently to the grass, turning back to defend against any who came her way. Pascal looked for the fallen sword and ran for it. Eshe and Lazarus stood guard where it fell. Mawarí leaped the gap before Pascal could reach the sword and the hyenas attacked him. Mawarí took Lazarus above his head and tore the beast in two. Bast pulled the god down and Pascal had time to grab the sword. Bring his lighter out he finally ignited it. It burned with a bright green fire and the scourges ran from him. Even the gods stepped back from this blade. He returned to the stones and withdrew a flask he had placed below Giving Stone and pored the liquid within on the still standing torches, lifting the others back upright. Using the sword he lit each of these in turn. They burst to life with massive green flames that reached high into the sky and all the demons and familiars stepped back from its potency. Basilio lifted Daphne from the bed and rushed back to the main house as fast as he could run with her. She was weak and fighting to remain awake. She tried to say something which he could not make it, but it sounded like his name.

Pascal rose heavily to his feet and pulled Jacob's bleeding body from the stone. Pascal pushed the Giving Stone against the Earning stone holding Aquilla, adjusting Aquilla's position so that only his upper body still remained on the stone he aligned the corpse's head at the intersection of the two stones. He pulled Jacob over and similarly arrange him across the stone Aquilla had been placed upon. He finally took Idalia and placed her on the second stone. He took each of their hands and clasped them together with each other so that each was holding one hand of the other two. Pascal then to a knife and slit the palms of each of them and replaced their hands together firmly. Mephisto screamed piercingly behind, leaping desperately only to be torn asunder by Bast. Pascal looked to the sky at the great moon glaring directly above. He dropped to his knees in the center of the two stones and drew the spear out of Aquilla's chest. Slicing his own palms he took the spear in his warm slick hands and, without hesitation, forced it down into his chest around his heart and piercing both of the stones below.

Distance ceased to be a concept as Pascal and Aquilla's souls projected through the cosmos, past dimensionality, outside time. They felt the tug of other souls and they called out to them. In answer thousands of lost souls taken through the ages in this beastly occultic ceremony assembled with them. Together they followed Aquilla who led them onward to the house of the so-called gods to wreck unholy vengeance upon them.

Behind them, where their corpses lay gathered in the cold of the night air, the crows and bats fell from the sky, Bast and the other familiars lay down never again stir, the gods fell over to dust and the stones shattered and grew dark.

As the years wound on and the world forgot of such madness, no clues of the accursed cult and their mad rituals remained. The crows had fallen to their rightful eternal sleep. The hyenas and Bast returned to the dust they should have become a century earlier as had the ancient gods. The stones, shattered and broken in the open field, were now nothing more than rubble.

All that remained was Idalia, Basilio and Daphne. Basilio had rescued Idalia and taken both her and Daphne to the hospital. They grew close as the only survivors left to believe what had truly happened that night. Basilio rebuilt Working Together in Atlanta for Idalia as a magnificent new modern center on the old plot. Elias came back to help and she even saw Damien stop by on occasion. Daphne helped her tend the gardens there and amidst the tomatoes and carrots ran Idalia's son Jacob. The joy of her life and the final gift from the lover who had been taken from her. She watched as Jacob picked a pretty rock and presented it to the baby girl that sat near Daphne. The baby smiled at him and took the stone in her hand, placing it towards her mouth before Daphne saw and reached over to pull it out. "Ah Ah, Idalia, no eat!" As she took it from the child she noticed it wasn't a rock, but a large decorative beetle, unmoving but seeming to be alive. She dropped it in shock and gave out a screech. Idalia came running to see what was up. "Look at this huge thing! I've never seen anything like it!"

Bending over to take a closer look Idalia answered, "Its a scarab beetle. Beautiful, but I've only ever seen them in books before. I have no idea how it got here." She laughed and reached down to touch its iridescent back. "So pretty, too bad its dead."

"Ewww, I can't believe you're touching it! Okay, enough excitement for now. C'mon kiddos, lets take these veggies inside and get them washed up." Daphne grabbed baby Idalia in her arm, taking one of the full bags of vegetables with her. Idalia took the second bag and led Jacob by the hand back to the new Walking Together center.

The beetle reflected the sun as they left, seeming to watch their retreat until the door to the center had closed behind them. Opening its shell, its wings began to beat. It flew a pass by the center, the large glass windows showing Daphne and Idalia at the sink washing the produce as the children played at their feet. It sailed on past the center and into the sky. It sensed new opportunity already awaiting not far away.

The End.